"Either you walk to that horse or I'll carry you,"

Hawk threatened.

Pride glistened in Amanda's eyes. "I am not getting on your horse and don't you dare touch me again."

"I'm not leaving you out here," he growled back.

"You have no choice. I am the master of my fate, and I'll make my own decision about who I want to be rescued by." Her jaw set in a firm line; she began to climb back up on the boulder.

Hawk's hand closed around her arm. "Damn you, Amanda," he snarled.

She turned to tell him to let go of her but before she could speak, his free hand cupped the back of her head and his mouth found hers.

Dear Reader,

Happy Valentine's Day! Love is in the air . . . and between every page of a Silhouette Romance novel. Treat yourself to six new stories guaranteed to remind you what Valentine's Day is all about. . . .

In Liz Ireland's *The Birds and the Bees,* Kyle Weston could truly be a FABULOUS FATHER. That's why young Maggie Moore would do *anything* to reunite him with his past secret love—her mother, Mary.

You'll find romance and adventure in Joleen Daniels's latest book, *Jilted!* Kidnapped at the altar, Jenny Landon is forced to choose between the man she truly loves— and the man she *must* marry.

The legacy of SMYTHESHIRE, MASSACHUSETTS continues in Elizabeth August's *The Seeker.*

Don't miss the battle of wills when a fast-talking lawyer tries to woo a sweet-tongued rancher back to civilization in Stella Bagwell's *Corporate Cowgirl.* Jodi O'Donnell takes us back to the small-town setting of her first novel in *The Farmer Takes a Wife.* And you'll be SPELLBOUND by Pat Montana's handsome— and magical—hero in this talented author's first novel, *One Unbelievable Man.*

Happy reading!

Anne Canadeo
Senior Editor

Please address questions and book requests to:
Reader Service
U.S.: P.O. Box 1325, Buffalo, NY 14269
Canadian: P.O. Box 1050, Niagara Falls, Ont. L2E 7G7

THE SEEKER
Elizabeth August

Silhouette
ROMANCE™
Published by Silhouette Books
America's Publisher of Contemporary Romance

To friends and neighbors in Wilmington, Delaware.
You will always have a place in my heart.

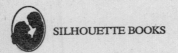 SILHOUETTE BOOKS

ISBN 0-373-08989-9

THE SEEKER

Copyright © 1994 by Elizabeth August

Printed in U.S.A.

ELIZABETH AUGUST

I've lived in both cities and small towns. I confess, I loved the small towns best. Every community, large or small, has its eccentrics and its secrets. But I've always felt that in a small town these elements become more focused. They add a touch of spice or, in some cases, discord, that seems to permeate the air and give the town a personality uniquely its own. When the thought occurred to me of creating an outwardly normal, small, conservative, rural community founded on a secret known to only a few but affecting the majority—a secret that in itself could be the basis for eccentricities—I found this too interesting a concept to resist. Thus, Smytheshire and its residents began to take form in my mind.

I have to admit, I've been shocked by how alive the people of Smytheshire have become to me. I've had a lot of fun creating these books. I hope you will enjoy reading them as much as I've enjoyed writing them.

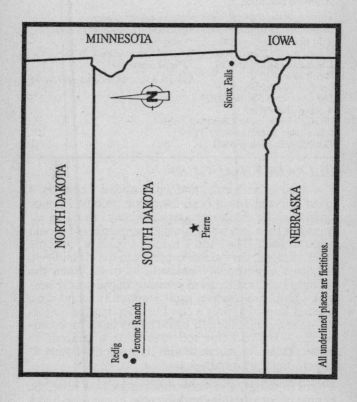

NORTH DAKOTA

MINNESOTA

IOWA

SOUTH DAKOTA

★ Pierre

Sioux Falls •

NEBRASKA

Redig •
• Jerome Ranch

All underlined places are fictitious.

Chapter One

"That's great. Just great," Amanda MacGreggor muttered. She'd pulled her car off to the side of the road, turned off the engine to conserve gas and was looking at the map draped across the steering wheel. She was lost. There was no doubt about that. And it was her own fault. She had simply been driving where the spirit moved her, so to speak. Now she was somewhere in one of the Dakotas or Wyoming or maybe even Montana. She wasn't sure which state or just where. What she *was* sure of was that she hadn't seen a town for miles or even another car for what seemed like ages. Night had fallen an hour ago and there were no lights anywhere in sight. All around her was desolate rolling prairie. To her left in the distance was the shadowy outline of ancient mountains.

Laying her forehead against the steering wheel, she groaned. How could she have behaved so stupidly? It was that diary her cousin Madaline Darnell had sent her that was responsible. The diary had belonged to one of their ancestors. It had talked about a druid heritage. And because of it, Amanda had decided to allow her instincts to lead her.

"Well, it wasn't entirely the diary's fault," she admitted, lifting her head. "My life is definitely lacking something." A full moon gave an eerie illumination to the landscape. "But I really doubt this is the way to find whatever that something is."

Suddenly she stiffened. She heard sobbing. Her gaze again swept the landscape. She saw no one. Wondering if she'd simply imagined the sound, she concentrated harder. No, it wasn't her imagination. She definitely heard sobbing—not wailing as if the person crying were injured or in immediate danger, but a quiet, frightened sort of weeping. "Seems as if I've found something," she murmured under her breath.

Reaching under her seat, she found the flashlight she kept there, then stepped out onto the road.

"This might not be the smartest action to take," she warned herself as she again scanned the darkened landscape. There were snakes, coyotes and who knew what else out there. She was a city girl, born and raised in Seattle, Washington. This land was alien to her. It occurred to her that maybe she should drive to the nearest house and seek help. But even as these thoughts played through her mind, she flicked on the light and jumped the small ditch on the side of the road. A barbed wire fence blocked her way.

"I hate fences, especially ones with barbs," she mumbled uneasily. "And I'm not dressed for this," she added, glancing down at the lightweight shirt and denim shorts she was wearing. The terrain in front of her was rugged, uncultivated land. During the day, she'd admired the wildflowers. Now all she was aware of were the patches of tall grass interspersed with thistles and brambles. She frowned down at her feet. "And these sneakers aren't going to protect me from any snakes."

Then she heard the sobbing again. Her attention returned to the fence. It was old and the wire was loose. Holding the third strand down, she managed to get through without getting caught or scratched. "Well, that's one obstacle conquered," she said, the sound of her own voice giving her courage as she made her way across the uneven terrain.

Amanda glanced over her shoulder. The road was no longer in sight. The realization of how far she'd come caused her nervousness to increase, but she couldn't turn back now. The sobbing was becoming more distinct. "Hello," she called out. "Do you need help?"

"Nana?" a child's voice cried out plaintively. "Nana?"

Amanda began jogging up the small hill to her right. As she reached the crest she saw a child coming toward her. The child's hair was blond and her shirt was white. The moonlight reflecting off the shirt and pale hair made her look ghostly. But that sobbing wasn't coming from a ghost, Amanda told herself as she slowed her pace.

Seeing her, the child froze. "Who are you?" she demanded. "I'm not supposed to talk to strangers."

Amanda had to admire the little girl's pluck. She was close enough now for Amanda to see that her shirt was torn in a couple of places. Obviously she'd had a difficult journey. Yet she wasn't ready to seek help from just anyone. "I'm sure it will be all right with your family if you talk to me," Amanda said soothingly, stopping where she was to encourage the child to trust her.

Tears began to roll down the small girl's cheeks. "I'm lost," she admitted between sobs.

Amanda judged the child's age to be somewhere around five. "I am, too. Maybe we can find our way back to civilization together," she suggested.

"We have to find Nana," the child demanded.

"Nana sounds like a good start." Amanda held out her hand. "Let's go find her."

For a moment longer the child hesitated, then nodded and approached Amanda, slipping her hand into Amanda's.

"My name's Amanda," Amanda introduced herself as she began to retrace her steps with the child in tow. She wasn't sure how she was going to find this Nana person, but she preferred making the attempt in her car as opposed to tramping through this scrubland any farther. "What's yours?"

"Juliet," the little girl replied.

"That's a pretty name," Amanda said with forced cheerfulness, playing her flashlight over the ground ahead of them as they walked. If the light didn't scare away any of the creatures she had no desire to meet, at least she'd see them first.

The sound of a horse's whinny broke the night air. Coming to a stop, Amanda looked over her shoulder. A horse and rider were approaching.

"Hawk and Loco." Juliet breathed the names in a voice laced with trepidation, her hold on Amanda's hand tightening.

Apparently I should have been afraid of more than just the four-legged beasts, Amanda thought, changing her hold on the flashlight so that she could use it as a club if necessary. She fervently hoped Loco was the name of the horse and not the man.

About six feet from them, the rider reined to a halt and drew a rifle out of a leather sling on his saddle.

Fear so intense she could hardly breathe swept through Amanda. Surely he wasn't going to hold a woman and small child at gunpoint, she thought frantically, yet the fear remained.

Pointing the weapon into the air, he fired two shots, then returned the weapon to its sling.

Obviously a search had been mounted for the child, and the shots were a signal to let others know he'd found her, Amanda realized. She gave a relieved sigh as he dismounted and walked toward them. But the relief was short-lived. A tenseness spread through her as the man remained silent. I'm letting this wilderness and the fact that I'm surrounded by darkness influence my judgment, she chided herself. This man was their rescuer. She had no reason to fear him. Then she noticed that the child's hold on her hand tightened even more. At least, I thought he was our rescuer, she amended.

She increased her grip on the flashlight as he came nearer. He was a big man. She guessed he stood better than six feet tall. The lithe way he moved gave evidence of physical strength. I cannot believe I got myself into this mess, she thought, fighting back a rush of panic.

The rider's gaze leveled on the little girl. "Juliet, are you all right?"

At least he finally said something, Amanda thought. His voice was cool and reserved, but she was sure she detected a note of concern.

"Yes," the little girl replied, pressing up against Amanda's leg as if seeking security.

The moonlight gave vague definition to his features, and Amanda saw the man frown. Then he shifted his gaze to her. "Who are you?" There was nothing friendly in either his expression or his voice.

"Amanda MacGreggor," she replied. She was tempted to turn the beam of the flashlight onto his face to get a more exact look at him but decided against it. If she was wrong about the concern in his voice and had to fight him, the moment of blindness she could cause by turning the light on him would be an advantage. Not wanting him to guess how much he unnerved her, she squared her shoulders and asked with equal coolness, "And who are you?"

"Hawk Stone."

Amanda noticed he didn't extend his hand in greeting. Just as well, she thought, preferring to keep as much distance between them as possible.

"She was lost like me," Juliet interjected, clearly feeling the need to explain Amanda's presence to this man.

Amanda felt more than saw his gaze intensify. The last thing she wanted was for him to think no one would miss her if she simply disappeared. "I have friends who are expecting me," she lied. "They'll call the police soon if they don't hear from me. They might even have called them already."

For a moment he regarded her in silence. She had the distinct feeling he was going to call her a liar. Her nerves were threatening to snap when he said, "Then we'd better get you to a phone."

Just getting away from him would be good enough, she thought. Aloud she said, "I was heading back to my car. I'm sure I can find a phone on my own." The pressure of Juliet's hold on her hand reminded her of her young companion. "And if you'll give me directions, I'll be glad to drop Juliet off at her home on my way."

Hawk's gaze swept the landscape. "Where is your car?"

"It's parked on the side of the road just over the next hill," she replied, already beginning to head toward it once again with Juliet.

"The road is in the other direction."

Amanda froze. She never lost her way when she was heading for her car. But just as she was about to assure him that he was the one who was wrong, her inner compass seemed suddenly to turn and she knew he was right. She couldn't believe she'd made a mistake like that. But then, she'd never been in a situation where she'd felt so threatened. "You're right," she said, and turned in the direction he'd indicated.

"I'd better take Juliet home." In two long strides, Hawk reached her and scooped the little girl up.

"I really don't mind driving her," Amanda insisted, continuing to hold on to the child's hand.

As if reading her thoughts, the cowboy regarded her dryly. "I'm not going to harm her."

Juliet's grip on Amanda slackened as her attention focused on the man. "You're really going to let me ride on Loco with you? Nana says no one but you can even get near that horse."

"He'll let you ride if I tell him to," Hawk assured the little girl.

Immediately Juliet let go of Amanda's hand.

Clearly the child was not only willing but excited about going with the cowboy, Amanda realized, feeling somewhat foolish. Standing back, she watched him swing the child up into the saddle then climb in behind her, wrapping one arm around Juliet's middle to hold her secure.

Once mounted, he extended his free hand toward Amanda. "Come on. I'll take you back to your car."

Amanda couldn't shake the unnerving effect this stranger was having on her. Juliet might be happy about accepting his aid, but she wasn't.

"Are you afraid of horses?" he asked.

An underlying challenge in his voice let her know he'd guessed that *he* was what really frightened her. Again her shoulders squared. "No." She grabbed his hand, slipped a foot in the stirrup he'd left open for her and swung herself up behind him.

"Hold on," he directed, picking up the reins.

Frantically she looked for something other than him to hold on to. There was nothing. As her arms circled him, she tried to concentrate on the child. But that wasn't easy. She was forced to brush against Hawk's back. It was rock hard. A rush of heat mingled with a chill, and her uneasiness increased. The sooner I get away from this place the better, she told herself.

"Is this your car?"

Hawk's voice caused her to start. He'd occupied so much of her attention she hadn't been aware of their surroundings. Now she saw that they had reached the fence beside her old Ford. "Yes," she answered quickly, nearly falling as she quickly dismounted.

"Wait a minute," he growled.

She'd reached for the strand of wire on the fence to hold it down so she could slip through. The urge to continue on to the other side was so strong it took all of her willpower to turn back.

"I'll hold the wire for you," he said, swinging down from the saddle.

Grabbing the top wire and putting his booted foot on the next wire, he held them open for Amanda to slip through. On the other side, she straightened and faced him. "Thanks," she said, glad to have the fence between them.

"Follow the road about two miles," he said. "There'll be a turnoff onto a dirt road to your right. That'll get you to the Jerome ranch. That's where I'll be taking Juliet. It's the closest phone, and I'm sure her grandmother would like to thank you." Then without waiting for any response, he got back on his horse behind Juliet and headed in the direction from which he'd come.

"I think I'll just keep driving," Amanda announced to the night as she climbed in behind the wheel of her car. But as she pulled out onto the road, she found herself arguing that she should make certain Juliet got home safely. In the next instant, she reminded herself that the child had seemed to know this Hawk Stone and hadn't been worried about going off with him.

But as she passed the road Hawk had told her to take, his image loomed in her mind. His face was more shadow than substance, and there'd been a coldness about him that made her uncomfortable. He wouldn't have told me how to find Juliet's grandmother if he hadn't meant to take the girl home, she reasoned.

Still, even as the argument against turning down that road continued in her mind, she hit the brake, shoved the car into reverse and backed up.

"Well, I did promise myself I would follow my instincts," she muttered as she drove down the hardpacked dirt road toward the Jerome ranch. "And my instincts are screaming at me to check on Juliet."

As the road wound around the base of a hill, ahead of her she saw the lights of a house. Details were hard to discern, but she could tell it was a large, two-story structure with a roofed front porch. The shadowed images of corrals and barns were also visible. Saddled horses were tied to two hitching posts below the porch, and a handful of people, mostly men, were standing around as if waiting for something. Their attention turned to her as she drove to the house and parked a short distance from the horses.

An older woman wearing a blouse, skirt and cow-boy boots, approached as Amanda climbed out of her car.

"Can I help you?" the woman asked.

Her tone made Amanda feel like an intruder. I should have kept driving, she berated herself. Aloud she said, "I found a little girl. She said her name was Juliet. Then a man named Hawk Stone came along. He insisted on bringing Juliet home. He also gave me directions to get here. He said there was a phone I could use." She didn't really have anyone to call, but it occurred to her that she could look in the phone book, discover where she was, find the nearest motel and make a reservation.

"Hawk is bringing Juliet home? Is my grand-daughter all right?" the woman demanded.

"Juliet is fine," Amanda assured her. The anxiety in the woman's voice again caused her to worry about the little girl.

"He's coming over the ridge now," a man's voice called out. Immediately the woman's attention shifted away from Amanda, and she started walking in the direction of the approaching horse and riders. The rest of the crowd moved with her and Amanda was deserted.

"Please forgive my mother's manners," a male voice said.

Well, not totally deserted, Amanda corrected as the speaker took a step closer. The rest of the men she'd seen had all been in Western garb. This one, however,

was dressed in a suit. Clearly not a ranch hand, she
decided. The light was dim but she could see that he
was boyishly handsome and guessed he was near her
own age of twenty-seven. "There's nothing to forgive. I can understand her concern for her granddaughter." The man smiled and extended his hand.
"Welcome to the Jerome ranch. I'm Jason Jerome,
Juliet's uncle. We heard the shots letting us know
she'd been found, but your assurance that she's fine is
a relief."

He was, she judged, about the same height as Hawk
Stone but less muscular. Accepting the handshake, she
noted that his palms were smooth. He also had the
most charming smile she'd seen in a long time. "I'm
Amanda MacGreggor."

"Miss or Mrs.?" he asked. The firm pressure he'd
used during the handshake had slackened, but he
continued to hold her hand and smile that charming
smile.

"Miss," Amanda replied. She'd been flirted with
before, but never with such expertise. This guy had to
be an expert at wrapping women around his little fin-
ger.

"It's a pleasure meeting you, Miss Amanda
MacGreggor." As he spoke, he released her hand
slowly, giving the impression he regretted ending the
contact. "I believe I heard you mention needing to use
a phone?"

Again Amanda found herself marveling at his tech-
nique. "Yes, thank you," she replied. The man was a
charmer, but she was too tired and too shaken by her
encounter with Hawk to pay him much attention.

"Juliet tells me you were lost, too?" Mrs. Jerome's voice interrupted as Amanda started to follow Jason to the house.

Amanda stopped and looked to her right to see the older woman approaching with the child walking beside her. The others who had gathered were mounting their horses and riding in the direction of the barns and outbuildings.

"Amanda found me and then we were lost together and then Hawk found both of us," Juliet said, as if this should clear up the whole business.

They had reached Amanda and the woman was now studying her guardedly. "I'm thankful you found my granddaughter, but what in the world were you doing wandering around on our land after dark?"

Amanda wasn't in the mood to give them her history. Instead, she said simply, "Like your granddaughter said, I was lost. I'd pulled over to the side of the road to study my map and try to figure out where I was when I heard Juliet crying."

The guardedness on the older woman's face relaxed. "I'm glad you did. I'm in your debt."

"I'd settle for the use of your phone book and phone," Amanda replied, then was forced to add, "and a little information about exactly where I am and where the nearest motel is so I can call and make reservations."

"The nearest motel is several miles down the road," Jason said before his mother could respond. "I'm sure you'd be much more comfortable here, and as my mother said, we are in your debt."

"Stay," Juliet encouraged, slipping her free hand into Amanda's.

"Of course you must stay the night," Mrs. Jerome said, taking the lead from her son and grandchild.

Although the woman's tone was not unfriendly, Amanda was sure Mrs. Jerome really didn't want her there. "I can't impose."

"It's no imposition," Jason insisted. "It's the code of the West to show hospitality to strangers in need of shelter for the night."

"Yes, you will have to stay. We can't send you out in the night to get lost again," Mrs. Jerome stated, clearly feeling trapped by her sense of hospitality. Without waiting for a response, she turned to a plump, middle-aged woman standing behind her. "Set an extra plate at the table, Pauline. I'll see that the yellow guest room is made ready."

As if this settled the matter, she turned her attention to the child beside her. "But the very first thing on my agenda is for you and me to have a serious talk about your not wandering off." As she spoke she started toward the house with the child in tow.

"The roast's cold and there ain't nothing I can do about it," the middle-aged woman grumbled as she followed Mrs. Jerome and Juliet. Glancing over her shoulder in Jason's direction, she added in a tone that held no compromise, "I'll be putting the food on the table in ten minutes."

"We were just about ready to sit down to dinner when we discovered Juliet's disappearance," Jason explained to Amanda, then added with an air of indulgence, "Don't let Pauline's grouching put you off. She's a marvelous cook. The meal will be delicious."

A protest, something to the effect that this was probably not a good time for them to have company, formed in Amanda's mind. But instead, she heard herself saying, "Leather would taste good to me at the moment."

Jason's charming smile broadened. "Good. Let me show you to your room."

As Amanda got her overnight bag out of the trunk, she was still finding it difficult to believe she'd agreed to stay. It was almost as if she had some unfinished business here, she thought. Then she scowled at herself. She was letting this notion of following her instincts get out of hand. She had no unfinished business here. Any lingering sensations she was experiencing were simply due to residual nervous tension from finding Juliet and encountering Hawk Stone.

However, she reasoned, the Jeromes did seem like nice people. Jason was certainly pleasant to be around, and she was exhausted. Besides, she would only be spending the night. She'd leave first thing the next morning. I'll even get my breakfast on the road so as not to disturb their early-morning routine, she promised herself as Jason took her bag and she followed him inside.

Chapter Two

Alone in her room, Amanda glanced at her reflection in the mirror. She knew she wasn't a beauty. But under normal conditions, she was reasonably pleasant to look at. She'd inherited her mother's ivory skin along with her father's auburn hair and brown eyes. Her nose was average in size and nicely shaped. Her lips were full, giving her more of a cute than pretty appearance.

Tonight, however, she looked a mess. Her long hair had been whipped around by the prairie wind until it stuck out in all directions. She'd chosen to wear no makeup. After all, she was supposed to be living a vagabond existence. Now, exhaustion made her skin especially pale, serving to emphasize the dark circles under her eyes.

She glanced at her makeup case. But as she started to reach for it, she stopped. She was too tired for a complete make-over. She was certain to smear the mascara or do something else that would make her look even worse. Besides, they'd all already seen her like this. Settling for a little lipstick and a quick hair brushing, she'd just finished with her hair and was weaving it loosely into a single braid at the back of her head when a knock sounded on her door. She answered it and found Mrs. Jerome waiting there.

In the light, Amanda could see that the woman had once been blond, but now her hair was turning gray. Her features were finely cut and nicely proportioned. She was slender and a good two inches taller than Amanda's five foot six. No, only an inch taller, Amanda corrected, noticing the heels of the woman's boots.

"I'll have your bed ready in a jiffy," Mrs. Jerome said, entering the room with an armload of linen.

"I really don't mind making it myself," Amanda said. "I appreciate your allowing me to spend the night."

"If we work together we can get the job done in half the time," the woman suggested.

"Agreed," Amanda replied.

Abruptly, as if just remembering something important, Mrs. Jerome shifted the sheets onto one arm and held out her hand. "I'm Gloria. I was so worried about my granddaughter I'm afraid I forgot my manners."

Amanda accepted the handshake. "I'm Amanda and I understand."

Minutes later, they were returning the bedspread to the freshly sheeted bed when a bell sounded. "We'd better get downstairs,'' Gloria said, giving the spread a final tuck, then moving toward the door. ''Pauline doesn't like people keeping her waiting when she's got dinner on. As it is, we're short on help just now. I don't need her throwing a tantrum and staging a strike.''

Amanda nodded knowingly. ''My mom always hates for us to linger when she's got dinner on the table,'' she said, following Gloria out of the room.

Juliet was waiting for them in the hall. Her long blond hair had been brushed, her face was washed, and she was wearing a fresh pair of shorts and a clean shirt. Seeing the child in the light for the first time, Amanda noticed that her eyes were blue like her grandmother's. She also had a similar pretty, delicately featured face.

''Come on,'' Juliet urged them, making a dash for the stairs. ''I'm hungry and I don't want to make Pauline mad.''

''You've already scared the life out of her and aged me at least ten years,'' Gloria said.

Juliet looked repentant. ''I've promised not to chase any more rabbits.''

''Or wander off on your own for any other reason,'' Gloria ordered.

''I will not leave the yard by myself,'' Juliet responded as if reciting an instruction that had been drilled into her.

''Good,'' Gloria said sternly, then waved her to proceed downstairs.

It was a comfortable house, warm and nicely furnished, Amanda thought as she followed the two females. But as she entered the dining room, a wave of uneasiness washed over her. She came to an abrupt halt.

Rising to greet them was Jason Jerome. Now that she'd seen his mother in the light, she could see the strong family resemblance. He was blond and blue-eyed like Gloria and Juliet. However, his handsome features were not delicate but decidedly masculine. Him she didn't mind encountering again.

It was the second man in the room who had caused her to tense. He was dressed in jeans, a blue broadcloth shirt and cowboy boots. His hair was raven in color, conservatively cut in front and around the ears but shoulder length in the back. His high cheekbones and the tint of his skin made her certain he had Native American blood running through his veins. Gray-green eyes offered a contrast to his darker features. He might be considered passably handsome, she decided, if his expression wasn't so cold and grim.

Out on the prairie, she hadn't gotten a really good look at Hawk Stone's face, but she knew without any doubt this man was him. Obviously they'd invited him to dine with them to show their appreciation. But if she'd known he was going to be there she would have thought twice about coming down to eat. However, she couldn't very well suddenly plead a headache and escape. Besides, it was ridiculous to let the man unnerve her so badly.

Gloria glanced toward Amanda. "I don't suppose I have to make any introductions. You've met both my son and Hawk."

"Yes," Amanda replied, forcing her legs to carry her forward.

"Sit here." Jason waved her to the chair he was standing behind.

She allowed him to seat her. He then took the chair at the head of the table. Gloria seated herself at the other end. Juliet sat down beside Amanda leaving Hawk the sole occupant of the opposite side of the table.

As they passed the food around, Amanda ordered herself to ignore the man seated across from her. Instead she remained intensely aware of him. He hadn't said anything since she and the other females had entered the room. He'd nodded politely toward them in acknowledgment of their presence, but maintained a cool, distant manner. Unable to stop herself, she glanced surreptitiously toward him. His steely gray-green eyes were studying her from behind a shuttered mask.

"You must have incredible hearing," he said, unexpectedly breaking his silence. "You were quite a distance from the road when I arrived and Juliet told me you'd only just found her."

She saw the challenge in his eyes and knew he didn't believe her story.

Jason frowned impatiently. "If she hadn't heard Juliet, why in the world would she have been wandering around on the prairie at that time of night?"

"I was wondering that myself," Hawk returned.

Gloria was now studying Amanda worriedly, clearly concerned that maybe she shouldn't have invited her to stay the night, after all. "Sound does travel peculiarly in these hills," she said as if trying to find some reason to believe Amanda.

In spite of his quick championship, even Jason was regarding her dubiously, Amanda noticed. She drew a resigned breath. She was going to have to tell them the truth. Maybe they'll give me a sandwich to eat before they send me on my way, she thought, glad she hadn't unpacked. "I didn't exactly hear Juliet in the conventional sense," she said. "I heard her in my mind. I find things. Usually not people, though. In fact, Juliet is the first person I've ever found."

Gloria looked confused. "But how did you know she was missing?"

"I didn't." Amanda had known they wouldn't understand. She didn't fully understand it herself. The talent was erratic and arbitrary. For most of her life she'd just assumed her little discoveries were based on luck or chance. It was the diary that had caused her to recognize her ability as an inherited trait. "I was driving along and I realized I was seriously lost. I pulled over to the side of the road to read my map. That's when I 'heard' Juliet. I followed the sound I heard in my mind until I heard her for real."

Amanda glanced toward the little girl who was continuing to eat without concern. That was what she liked about children, she thought. They were so innocent, their minds so open. Clearly Juliet didn't find anything threatening or unusual in what she was saying.

Her gaze shifted to Hawk. She expected him to be watching her with cynical disbelief and to make a snide comment implying she might be one brick short of a full load. Instead, although his expression remained coolly distant, he said, "My grandfather spoke of knowing of people with that ability."

"It could be very useful," Jason remarked. His gaze leveled on Amanda. "How does it work? Can you simply think of something that's missing and see where it is?"

Amanda had grown used to expecting skepticism, but Jason didn't sound skeptical. He seemed sincerely curious. "I'm not sure exactly how it works," she confessed. "Sometimes people tell me they've lost something and I'll see it, but other times I just draw a blank. I don't seem to have any control over what I find or when I find it. It just happens."

Gloria was now regarding her thoughtfully. "How intriguing."

Amanda's gaze shifted from Gloria to Jason. She was both relieved and amazed that they appeared to believe her. It was, she realized, as if Hawk's confirmation of people with her kind of talent had made her claim legitimate in the eyes of the others.

"Hawk has lost a gold mine," Juliet said, looking across the table at the man opposite her with a hint of awe in her eyes, as if she found him intriguing but a little scary at the same time. "I heard my mother and Uncle Jason talking about it once. They said if he found it, he could buy this ranch and then we'd all be able to live in peace."

"Juliet, we all live in peace now," Gloria said tersely.

Juliet looked mildly disgruntled, and for a moment Amanda thought she was going to refute her grandmother's statement. Instead, she returned to eating her dinner.

Watching Hawk, Amanda thought that living in peace with him was highly unlikely.

He frowned as if he found the subject of the mine irritating. "The mine is merely a legend."

Gloria nodded in agreement. "If that mine had actually existed, it would have been found by now. Speckled Owl would have found it. From what I've heard, he walked every inch of that land of his a hundred times."

"My great-grandfather *did* search," Hawk confirmed. "I even searched with him when I was a child. But that's all the mine is—a child's and an old man's fantasy. Something to go looking for to pass idle hours. I have no idle hours now."

Amanda suddenly found herself picturing an old Indian accompanied by a young boy slowly wandering across this desolate land. The old Indian was talking and the boy was listening with a serious, intense expression. The sharpness of the image surprised her.

"Have you called your friends yet?"

The image vanished. Looking toward her questioner, Amanda saw the cold mockery in Hawk's eyes. Anger spread through her. He knew she'd lied to him out on the prairie, and he found it amusing that he'd frightened her into lying! "No."

"You were on your way to visit friends when you got lost?" Jason asked solicitously.

"They must be worried sick," Gloria said with concern. "You should call them immediately. Tell them you're at the Jerome ranch. We're southwest of Redig."

Amanda flushed with embarrassment. "When I said I was lost, I meant it. I'm really lost." She paused. "Is Redig in Montana, North Dakota, South Dakota or Wyoming?"

"South Dakota," Jason replied.

Gloria frowned reprimandingly. "Your friends' instructions must have been very badly given."

Hawk, Amanda noted, had remained silent, watching her in a calculating manner that suggested he'd made a bet with himself about whether or not she would lie again. Ignoring him, she turned to Gloria. "The truth is I wasn't on my way to visit friends. I got myself lost all on my own."

Out of the corner of her eye Amanda saw Jason glance at Hawk. The frown on his face showed he'd guessed Hawk had frightened her into claiming to have friends waiting for her. Turning his attention to her, he smiled warmly. "And where were you heading?"

"No place in particular."

"This is a long way from anywhere to be out for a drive," Hawk observed, studying her as if he didn't think it was wise to really trust her.

She met his gaze levelly. "I simply decided to see a little of the world, so I packed a few things and took off."

Gloria smiled as if she finally understood. "You're on vacation."

Amanda considered letting this explanation stand. But lies had a way of catching up with people, and she rebelled against having another one exposed in front of Hawk. "Not exactly. I woke up one morning with the strongest feeling that something important was missing in my life. I was bored with my work. I felt caged in by family and friends." Not wanting to give them the wrong impression, she added quickly, "My parents are very nice people and so are my friends. I just felt the need to get away on my own for a while. I've had a good job for the past couple of years and managed to save some money. When I was in college I helped support myself by working as a waitress. I figured with that work experience I could find temporary jobs along the way and just travel where my mood took me."

For a moment, no one said anything. Sort of like the shocked reaction she'd gotten from her parents when she'd first announced her intentions to them.

It was Gloria who broke the silence. "Well, it's always good to get the wanderlust out of your system before you get saddled with responsibilities," she said. "Men do that all the time. There shouldn't be anything wrong with a woman doing it."

"To the liberated female," Jason said, raising his glass.

She saw the gleam in his eyes. Clearly he thought she might be easily available. Now was as good a time as any to put that idea out of his mind. "I've got too strong a conservative streak to really be considered liberated," she said. "I see myself more as a seeker than an aimless wanderer."

Jason's smile returned to being politely friendly. "Then here's to your success in finding what you seek."

"Thank you," she replied, glad he'd gotten the message and accepted it well.

Gloria cast her son a glance that suggested he should be more subtle in the future. Then she turned her attention to Amanda. "You said you had a college degree. What did you major in?"

"Business management."

"Too bad we don't need any help with the books," Jason lamented charmingly.

The man didn't give up easily, Amanda mused.

"But we do need help around the house," Gloria said, her manner becoming businesslike.

Amanda noticed Hawk glance toward Gloria warningly, but either the woman didn't see him or she chose to ignore him.

"The girl who usually comes in during the days to help got married and moved away, and I haven't found anyone to replace her yet," Gloria continued. "I've invited half the county to a party, and with Juliet here, to boot, I'm getting panicky. When Jasmine, my daughter, called and asked if Juliet could stay with me for a couple of weeks so Jasmine and her husband could go on a romantic vacation, I said certainly. I'm always glad to spend time with my granddaughter. But I'd forgotten how busy a five-year-old can keep a person. If you'd be interested in a maid's position for a while, you're welcome to stay. Your salary wouldn't be much, but you'd have free room and board. Pauline's rooms off the kitchen are the only separate quarters we have for live-in help. The wranglers, of course, stay in the bunkhouse, but that's men's territory. You'd have to remain in the yellow guest room.

There's a full bath on each end of the second floor, but you will have to share.''

Living on a ranch for a while could be fun, Amanda thought. She also had to admit that knowing Hawk didn't want her to have this position was egging her on. "Thanks," she said. "I'll take the job."

Juliet grinned at her. Gloria smiled with relief. Jason looked pleased. Only Hawk greeted her decision with cold disapproval.

But then, he doesn't matter, Amanda told herself. He doesn't live here. He's merely a dinner guest.

A few hours later Amanda sat in the upholstered chair in her room, staring at the closed door. How could she have made such a gross mistake? Not only did Hawk live here, he was ranch foreman and part owner! She'd found this out from Pauline.

After dinner, Amanda had insisted on beginning her new job immediately by helping the cook with the dishes. Both Pauline and Gloria looked exhausted, and Amanda knew she would feel guilty if she simply gave in to her own weariness and went to bed.

As Pauline had washed the pots and pans and handed them to Amanda to dry, she'd said, "Working here won't be hard as long as you remember a few simple rules. The downstairs study is Mr. Jason's domain. He has a lot of confidential information lying around on his desk. You shouldn't open any of his files or read any of whatever is lying around. You just dust around everything and don't pay it any mind."

Amanda had learned during dinner that Jason was a lawyer. That occupation, she thought, suited him well. "I make it a practice not to invade other people's privacy," she'd assured Pauline.

"Then there's Hawk."

Amanda had been in the process of putting a pan away. She froze in midmotion, then turned to look at the cook's back.

"The upstairs study is his," Pauline said, continuing to scrub the pan in the sink. "All the paperwork for the ranch is there. He keeps his desk neater than Mr. Jason keeps his. But I wouldn't go moving anything around. He don't like anyone bothering his things. And you should keep that in mind when you're cleaning his room. If you pick up something to dust under it, put it back where you found it."

"Hawk Stone lives here?" Amanda had choked out, still finding this disclosure hard to swallow.

Pauline glanced toward her questioningly. "Didn't anyone tell you? He's foreman and one of the heirs to the ranch."

"Mrs. Jerome sort of left that part out," Amanda replied. The moment she'd gotten up from the table and assumed her position as maid, Amanda had immediately returned to addressing Gloria and Jason Jerome in more formal terms. And now Hawk Stone would have to be added to her list of people she was to treat with deference.

"Hawk is Mrs. Jerome's illegitimate stepson," Pauline had elaborated. Her tone became stern. "I ain't a gossip, but everyone knows the story. And as long as you're going to be here for a while, you should know so's you won't go saying the wrong thing."

I've already said the wrong thing, Amanda thought. I accepted this job. "It would be prudent for me to know what not to say to people," she agreed.

Pauline nodded. "Ain't no sense in touching sore spots unnecessarily." Picking up another pan, she began scrubbing it as she spoke. "Hawk's mother was Speckled Owl's granddaughter. She was Sioux and lived with her family on the reservation. One summer Speckled Owl fell and hurt his hip. He refused to leave his home so she came to nurse him. I don't really know the details about how she and Jack Jerome got together, but they did. Their relationship was short-lived, though. Nobody even knew about it at the time. Jack's father, Eric Jerome, would've had a fit. He hated Indians, especially Sioux, and Speckled Owl in particular. The two of them had fought over land boundaries off and on for years. Speckled Owl owned eighty-nine acres surrounded on all sides by Jerome property. Eric tried to buy it, but the old Sioux refused to sell. He was, I suppose you could say, a thorn in Eric Jerome's side.

"Anyway, as soon as Speckled Owl was able to get around on his own again, Mercy Stone, Hawk's mother, went back to the reservation. It's my guess she didn't discover she was pregnant until after she was home. By that time, Jack had gotten himself engaged to Mrs. Jerome. I figure Mercy had her pride and refused to come back here and insist he do the right thing by her. Instead, she had the baby without ever telling him about it."

Pausing, Pauline turned to Amanda. "Jack was a good man. He would have given the boy his name."

Returning to scrubbing her pans, she continued. "Anyway, it was eight years later that Mercy came to the ranch with the boy. She was dying of cancer. Her parents couldn't afford to raise her son along with the rest of their children. Mercy had married, but her husband had never accepted Hawk. To make matters worse, the man she married was unable to father any children. That made him even more bitter toward the boy."

Pauline lowered her voice, clearly not wanting to be overheard. "Rumor has it that Mercy's husband never called Hawk by name. He always called him Half-breed, and he wasn't above striking the boy."

Amanda frowned thoughtfully. "I guess that could explain why Hawk's so grim."

"That's only half of it." Pauline shook her head. "Mercy didn't give Jack a choice. She simply left the child here. Of course, there was nothing else she could've done. She died barely a month later. The fact that the child had been conceived before Jack and Gloria Jerome were married is probably the only reason their marriage survived the trauma of this unexpected offspring. Jack had some real making-up to do, I can tell you."

Glancing at Amanda, Pauline added quickly, "I'm not saying Gloria Jerome wasn't good to the boy. She was. It was Eric Jerome who caused the real trouble. He was still alive then and this ranch was his. Jack lived here with his family and ran the place, but it belonged to Eric, and the old man refused to even recognize Hawk's existence."

A reproving expression spread over Pauline's face. "I've never seen a grown man act like such an ass. He'd leave a room if the boy entered and refused to allow the child to sit at the table with the rest of the family. This ranch was as much a part of Jack Jerome as an arm or leg. He couldn't leave, and he knew it wasn't healthy for the boy to grow up in such a hostile atmosphere. So he struck a deal with Speckled Owl. Hawk would live with his great-grandfather and Jack would pay all his son's expenses and provide money for a woman to come in daily and cook and clean for the old man and the boy. Speckled Owl agreed."

Pauline paused to put aside the pan she'd just finished cleaning and picked up another. "When Hawk was eleven, Eric died. Jack wanted the boy to move back into this house at that time, but Hawk insisted on staying with his great-grandfather. By then Speckled Owl was well into his nineties and not getting around too good. He died when Hawk was fourteen. That's when the boy moved in here and Jack taught him ranching."

"You left out the part about how I got suspended from school when I was nine and never went back."

Amanda jerked around to discover Hawk by the back door. He was standing with his shoulders leaned against the wall and his arms folded in front of him. The hard set of his jaw caused a chill to run through her.

"It ain't polite to sneak up on people, and it's especially impolite to eavesdrop," Pauline admonished, clearly unruffled by his unexpected presence.

"I thought gossiping was impolite," he returned dryly.

Pauline tossed him a haughty glance. "I figured that if Amanda was going to stay for a while, she should know the lay of the land so she wouldn't go doing or saying anything to embarrass herself or anyone else." Her expression became self-righteous. "Why, she didn't even know you lived here in this house."

Hawk's gaze leveled on Amanda. "I suppose you thought I had a tepee out in the hills someplace."

The icy mockery was back in his voice, but Amanda refused to be intimidated by him again. "Actually I pictured something more like a lean-to with a campfire in front and rattlesnake skins hanging on the poles."

For a moment Pauline looked stunned, then she grinned at Hawk. "You asked for that one."

One corner of his mouth quirked up in a smile. "I did," he conceded, then straightening away from the wall, he strode out of the kitchen.

"I didn't think he could smile," Amanda said. Realizing she'd spoken aloud, she flushed.

"He doesn't much. Social graces ain't one of his strong points," Pauline replied. "Truth is, he don't seem to have much use for people in general. When he first came here, he and I went a couple of rounds. Even at that young age, he was set in his ways and stubborn as a mule. But I've never been one to let anyone reign over me or my kitchen. He and I came to a quick understanding." Regret laced her voice. "I figured he needed a friend so I tried to be one to him. But he refused to take to me. Fact is, he's never taken to anyone here, really. Eventually he and his dad formed a mutual respect for each other, but I don't think there was ever any emotional ties. As for him and the rest of the family, they all tolerate one another in a sort of peaceful coexistence.''

It again had occurred to Amanda that she would never have used the word ''peaceful'' in any sentence referring to Hawk, but she didn't say this aloud. Instead, she'd shifted the subject to the dishes, suggesting they finish them and go to bed. Pauline had readily agreed.

Now Amanda was sitting in her room staring at the door. She'd never thought of herself as a coward. She'd dealt with difficult people before and never allowed them to dissuade her from a job she'd set her mind to. But Hawk's presence disturbed her in a way she'd never experienced before. He created an uneasiness within her that permeated every fiber of her being. I'll think of leaving here as a strategic retreat, she decided. Tomorrow morning I'll tell Mrs. Jerome I've reconsidered the job offer and decided not to accept it, after all. Then I'll thank her and be on my way. Having made this decision, she went to bed.

Chapter Three

"I never know whether to consider Hawk a blessing or a curse," Gloria Jerome was saying.

Amanda had come downstairs to find the woman and tell her of her decision to leave. Gloria was in Jason's study, and the door was open just enough for the voices of those inside to be heard in the hall. Amanda raised her hand to knock and let them know she was there when a prickling on the back of her neck caused her to glance over her shoulder.

Hawk was standing a foot away.

"I will be forever grateful to him for finding Juliet," Gloria continued. "But I know he's going to scare Miss MacGreggor off, and I really do need some help at the moment."

"Am I going to scare you off, Miss MacGreggor?" Hawk asked, keeping his voice low so as not to alert those in the study to his and Amanda's presence.

There was mockery in the depths of his eyes, as if he'd guessed her purpose for being there. Pride caused her shoulders to stiffen. She refused to allow herself to be chased off by a bully. "No," she replied in equally hushed tones.

The door of the study was suddenly swung fully open. "Hawk! Amanda!" Gloria gasped in surprise.

"I was just coming to ask what you wanted me to do this morning," Amanda said, feeling trapped. She told herself it was foolish to stay here just to prove to Hawk she wasn't afraid of him. But she couldn't allow herself to appear a coward by leaving, either.

"Good morning, Amanda." Jason smiled with welcome as he rose from his desk and approached the door. "I hope you slept well."

"Yes, thank you," she replied, trying to concentrate on Jason and ignore Hawk. But ignoring the imperious cowboy wasn't easy. She could feel him watching her, as if his gaze was a physical touch.

"Juliet's in the kitchen helping with breakfast. We should go rescue Pauline before her patience is all used up." Gloria started down the hall as she spoke, motioning for Amanda to follow.

Amanda had the distinct impression the woman was trying to get her away from Hawk as quickly as possible. Glad for any excuse to escape his presence, Amanda readily followed Gloria's lead.

Behind her she heard Hawk saying to Jason, "You have some papers I need to look at?"

"Yes," was Jason's terse reply.

They sounded like adversaries rather than two men discussing a mutual business arrangement, Amanda thought. But then, Hawk seemed to treat nearly everyone as an adversary. She couldn't fault Jason for being brusque.

Fifteen minutes later, Amanda was in the kitchen making orange juice. Pauline was mixing bread dough to be baked later that day, and Gloria had taken Juliet upstairs to change the child out of her pajamas and into play clothes.

The door that led into the hall suddenly flew open. Hawk strode through the kitchen without a word and out the back door.

"Guess he doesn't want any breakfast," Amanda said, thinking she'd never seen a man look so angry.

"Hawk ate ages ago," Pauline replied, frowning worriedly at the door he'd just gone through. "'Course he usually stops by for a couple of my homemade muffins about now."

Looking out the back window, Amanda watched Hawk striding toward the barns. "I guess what he and Jason had to discuss made him more irritable than usual."

"They probably had another quarrel about selling the ranch." Kneading her bread, Pauline continued to frown. "Jack Jerome loved this ranch. He knew Jason and Jasmine—that's Juliet's mother—didn't feel the same way he did about it. And Mrs. Jerome has never shown any real attachment to it, either. Hawk was the only one who learned to love this place as much as Jack. So, Jack left a pretty complicated will in an attempt to ensure it would stay intact and in the family after his death. The ranch was left to his wife for the duration of her life, as long as it isn't sold. And it can't be sold without the consent of her and all three children, unless it starts to lose money—then the majority rules. If it is sold, then she and each of the children will receive a fourth of the proceeds. When she dies, the ranch goes equally to the three children. Again, they can't sell it unless all three agree or the ranch starts losing money. Then the majority rules. During Mrs. Jerome's lifetime and afterward, Hawk is to remain foreman and make all the business decisions relating to the running of the ranch. As long as he keeps the place going at a profit, or just breaks even during the rough years, the others can't interfere."

Pauline shook her head. "It ain't fair. Jason has his law practice. Jasmine's husband has a good job. And both children were left a nice lump sum of money by their father. Mrs. Jerome's got plenty of money, too. Jack had good solid investments and left a large insurance policy in her name. She gets all the profits from the ranch, too. Hawk works for a salary. If she doesn't want to live here, she could afford to buy a place and live in town, and so could Jason."

Amanda studied the cook narrowly. "You like Hawk," she said, finding it difficult to believe anyone honestly could.

"He's rough on the outside, but he's got a good heart," Pauline declared. "He just don't let anyone see it. It was my sister who looked after him and Speckled Owl. She told me the boy could be a hellion, but he obeyed the old man and looked after him. And I seen for myself how careful he took care of his great-grandfather."

Straightening from her kneading, Pauline looked Amanda in the eye. "As for this ranch, not even Jack Jerome could have worked any harder than Hawk does to keep it running."

A bell sounded from the dining room. "I guess they're ready for breakfast," Amanda said, moving toward the door to wait on the table. She still found it difficult to believe Hawk could inspire what actually sounded like loyalty from the cook. Maybe Pauline was just afraid of losing her job and not being able to find another if the ranch was sold, she reasoned as she entered the dining room. Then she put Hawk out of her mind as she approached Gloria Jerome to ask her what she wanted for breakfast.

"Why don't you go unpack the rest of your things," Pauline suggested. "Then I'll take you on a cleaning tour of the house."

After having attended the family during their meal, Amanda had just finished eating her own breakfast and was carrying her dishes to the sink. "I'll just bring my suitcases in from the car," she replied. "I can unpack later."

The bright morning sun greeted her cheerfully as she left the house. Scanning her surroundings, she had to admit there was something invigorating about this land. She drew a deep breath. The smell of horses and cattle mingled with the scent of the prairie grasses. A surprisingly soothing yet stimulating odor, she thought. But as she started toward her car, the sense of peace that had come over her vanished.

Hawk was riding toward her on Loco. The black stallion looked larger and fiercer than he had the night before. But it wasn't the horse that caused her to tense, she admitted. It was the rider. Ignore him, she ordered herself, angry that she'd allowed Hawk to destroy her enjoyment of this beautiful morning. Pretending not to notice him, she continued on to her car. Still, out of the corner of her eye, she couldn't stop herself from watching him.

He rode to the steps leading to the front porch and dismounted. Gloria was seated in a rocking chair on the porch, knitting. Juliet was nearby, playing with her dolls.

Mounting the steps, Hawk bid a polite good-morning to Gloria, then turned to Juliet. "I've brought you a gift," he said, approaching the child and squatting to bring himself closer to eye level with her.

Amanda expected the little girl to make a dash for her grandmother, but instead, Juliet rose and stood facing him. Amanda had the impression the child was surprised Hawk was paying any attention to her. "Thank you for letting me ride Loco last night," she said.

"You're welcome," Hawk replied.

Amanda couldn't see his face, but she noticed that his voice actually held a gentler note than usual. As for Juliet, Amanda could see her face and noted that the child seemed more fascinated by the man than afraid. Moths are fascinated by flames, too, she mused, and look what happens to them when they get too close. Realizing that it wasn't the child's but her own continued inability to ignore Hawk that had caused this thought, she frowned and ordered herself to concentrate on getting her luggage out of the trunk of her car.

"My grandfather taught me to make whistles when I was a boy," Hawk was saying. "I made this one especially for you. You cover one or two of the holes, depending on what kind of sound you want, and then blow."

Amanda found herself unable to resist looking toward the porch. She saw Hawk hanging what looked like a whittled wooden stick, about four inches long and strung on a leather strap, around Juliet's neck.

"The next time you wander off, I want you to stay in one place and blow this whistle," he instructed. "That way we can find you more easily, and the sound will scare off any wild animals."

Juliet put the wooden instrument to her lips and blew. A shrill, loud noise issued.

"Promise me you'll wear it all the time you're here," Hawk said.

Juliet smiled brightly, clearly pleased with her gift. "I promise."

Hawk nodded, then rising, he started to leave the porch.

"Thank you, Hawk," Gloria said.

He paused to look at her. "Juliet is my niece. I wouldn't want anything bad to happen to her."

The gruff sincerity in Hawk's voice shook Amanda. He honestly cared about the child's welfare. And because he felt he had to remind Gloria that he was a member of the family, Amanda felt an unexpected wave of sympathy for him.

Watching him out of the corner of her eye, she saw him continue down the steps. But he didn't mount Loco and ride away as she'd expected. Instead, he headed toward her.

"I'll give you a hand with your luggage," he said as he neared the car.

In spite of her more positive image of him, he still made her uneasy. "That's really not necessary."

His gaze had fallen on the overnight bag she'd carried out to the car earlier that morning. From the sudden confusion on his face, she knew he remembered she'd taken it inside the night before. "I thought you were staying," he said.

She met his gaze levelly. "I am."

As the truth dawned on him, a flicker of amusement flashed in his eyes. "But earlier this morning you weren't planning to. It seems Gloria owes me a second thank-you." He raised a mocking eyebrow. "But isn't it a little immature to change your plans simply to prove you're not afraid of me?"

"I'm not staying to prove you don't scare me," she lied, refusing to give him the satisfaction of knowing he could have any influence over her life. "I'm staying because Mrs. Jerome honestly needs help." Grabbing her overnight bag and one of her suitcases, she headed for the house.

Behind her, she heard the trunk lid slam. Glancing over her shoulder, she saw Hawk starting to follow with the other suitcase. She forced a smile as she passed Gloria and Juliet. All the way up the stairs, she experienced a most uncomfortable prickling sensation on the back of her neck. But as she entered her room, it ceased. Turning, she saw Hawk put her suit-case down in the hall just outside the door of her room. Before she could issue a cool thank-you, he turned and left.

"That man can be truly irritating," she muttered as she retrieved the second suitcase.

A little later she admitted that if she'd known how close she'd be living to him, she would definitely have thought twice about staying.

When Amanda had gone back to the kitchen after unpacking, Pauline had stopped in the midst of cook-ing and given her a quick tour of the house, while ex-plaining what cleaning needed to be done in each room and what the weekly schedule was. That was when Amanda had discovered that Hawk's rooms were just across the hall from hers. The staircase formed a di-viding line, and the rest of the family occupied the other half of the floor.

That was another thing Mrs. Jerome had neglected to mention when she'd offered her this job. Amanda grimaced as she glanced over her shoulder at the bathroom located next to her room. Last night, she'd been too tired to care whom she was sharing it with. This morning, she'd noticed the shaving equipment but just assumed it belonged to Jason. Not until Pau-line had given her the tour had she realized what the true arrangements were. Hawk was her bathroom mate.

Now she stood with her hand on the knob of his study door.

"Just don't touch any of the papers on Hawk's desk," Pauline had cautioned before leaving Amanda to straighten, dust and vacuum the rooms on the second floor.

"I'd prefer not to even enter his rooms," Amanda grumbled to the empty hall as she forced herself to turn the knob. She'd finished cleaning the rest of the floor. His rooms were all that were left. She couldn't avoid them any longer. Yet, in spite of her desire to avoid anything to do with Hawk Stone, she was curious about how he lived.

"I'm the maid. I have to do this," she muttered as she opened the door and entered. Still, as she crossed the threshold, she felt like an intruder. "I've got to stop letting that man unsettle me this way," she admonished herself. But as she moved around the room, she was acutely aware that this was his domain.

The furnishings were nothing out of the ordinary. There were a couple of overstuffed upholstered chairs. A large rug covered most of the hardwood floor. The desk was a flat-top style made of maple, with the usual accessories: a pencil holder with several pens and pencils, an In tray and an Out tray, a blotter, a telephone and a lamp. Two wooden bookshelves were behind the desk. They held rows of ledgers along with tomes containing information on the various aspects of ranching: crops, cattle breeding and so on. All in all, this could have been any rancher's study, she thought. But it wasn't just any rancher's study. It was Hawk's, and that made her tense. Working carefully, she made certain that anything she moved was replaced in its exact former location.

Next came his bedroom. Her first impression was that it was neater than the others. Then she realized that wasn't a fair assessment. Juliet's room, which had obviously been the nursery, was cluttered with toys, but the bed had been made and there were no clothes lying around. The bed in Mrs. Jerome's room had also been made and her clothes put away. Jason's bed was the only one of the three that hadn't been made, but the rest of his things had been in fairly neat order.

His things! The mementos and other objects that gave personality to a room—that was where the difference lay, she realized. The other rooms had seemed more cluttered because there were personal items everywhere. In Juliet's room there had been toys. In Gloria Jerome's room there had been a collection of perfume bottles on her dressing table and some porcelain thimbles on her dresser, along with several photographs. In Jason's room, photos of friends had been stuck in the sides of his mirror, and there had been a wooden bowl filled with a clutter of boyhood objects, from a fishing lure to a small penknife.

But Hawk's room was starkly devoid of the kind of personal items that placed his mark on this space. Anyone could have lived here. Even the decor was void of personality. Plain blue curtains matched the blue quilted bedspread. The walls were white with blue trim. Granted, there was a handful of change on top of the dresser, but that was the only real evidence that someone actually used the room.

She'd expected something more. She'd experienced a sensation of his presence in his study. She'd expected his room to contain that same sense of his occupancy. But there was nothing about this bedroom that made it Hawk's room. Or maybe, she reasoned, this room did symbolize the real Hawk—a cold, empty man.

Abruptly she stiffened. She hadn't heard him approaching, but she knew he was there. Turning, she saw him standing in the doorway, an expression of irritation on his face. "I was just getting ready to vacuum," she said, to justify her presence in his room.

"I need to get a few things," he growled, brushing past her. From the closet, he pulled out an old worn pair of saddlebags.

Now those, Amanda thought, *did* look like something he'd own. As she watched, he grabbed a shirt and pair of jeans from the closet, rolled them together and stuffed them into one of the bags. She caught him glancing in her direction, and the irritation in his expression increased. A sudden suspicion crossed her mind. "If you're leaving because I agreed to stay, then I'll leave," she snapped.

He paused to regard her dryly. "Whether you stay or leave is of no consequence to me."

Of course it wouldn't be, she admonished herself, feeling like a fool for even mentioning such a possibility. It was just that the man rattled her. For the umpteenth time, she ordered herself to ignore him, but instead, she continued to watch him as he strode toward the dresser.

She thought he looked unsteady as he rounded the bed. Then she noticed the beads of perspiration on his forehead. The temperature in the house wasn't warm enough to cause him to break into a sweat. As he grabbed some clothing from a drawer in the dresser, her gaze narrowed on his reflection in the mirror in front of him. There was a glazed look in his eyes.

"You don't look too good," she said.

Ignoring her, he shoved the drawer of the dresser closed. Then tossing the saddlebags over his shoulder, he headed for the door.

She told herself that whatever he chose to do was none of her business. Still, she heard herself saying, "You look like you should be going to bed, instead of going off on whatever excursion you're planning."

When he continued toward the door as if he hadn't even heard her, she scowled at his back. Well, if he wants to be that way, let him, she thought.

Gloria Jerome suddenly appeared in the doorway, blocking Hawk's exit. "Pauline says you've got that flu that's been going around," she said. "She also told me she thinks you're planning to go to your place." Her voice took on a sharp edge. "Obviously she's right."

"You know I don't like having people around when I don't feel well," Hawk replied, placing his hands on her shoulders and gently but firmly moving her to one side.

"You can't go off by yourself. You need someone to look after you," she protested.

Hawk's gaze leveled on her. "I can take care of myself. I always have."

The frown on her face deepened. "This flu is dangerous. Harry Calhoun almost died."

"Harry's always had a weak constitution," Hawk replied, brushing past her and continuing down the hall.

Gloria turned to Amanda, her expression asking for help.

Amanda told herself that Hawk was not her responsibility, but even as this thought filled her mind, she stepped out into the hall and called out to his departing back, "You're being unreasonably stubborn." As usual Hawk ignored her.

Curtly she told herself that his actions were none of her business. But when he reached the stairs and she saw him grab the banister to maintain his balance, a sharp jab of concern rocked her. Quickly following him, she reached him as he started down the hall to the kitchen.

"You're in no condition to go anywhere," she said sharply, placing her hand on his arm to stop him.

His shirt was rolled up to the elbow and as her hand contacted his skin, she was shaken by how hot he felt. "You're burning up!"

Jerking free, he continued into the kitchen. "Have you got that food ready for me?" he asked Pauline, not even pausing as he continued to the back door.

"No." The cook placed herself in front of the door, barring his way. "You look like death. You go straight back upstairs to your room and get into bed."

He scowled fiercely. Using the same maneuver he'd used with his stepmother, he moved her out of his way and left the house.

"It ain't no use trying to stop him," Pauline said as Amanda started out the door after him.

"As a child, he was difficult. As a man, he's impossible," Gloria said, joining the two women at the back door.

Loco was waiting outside. The women watched as Hawk tossed the saddlebags over the stallion's back, then swung himself up into the saddle and rode off.

"I should have known I couldn't talk any sense into him," Pauline lamented. "I should have fixed that bag of food he wanted. He'd not going to have anything to eat up at his place."

Gloria breathed a sigh. "Someone's going to have to go up there and watch over him."

"He don't like anyone up there," Pauline warned.

Gloria nodded. "He is somewhat inhospitable when it comes to visitors at his place."

Amanda had difficulty believing Hawk could be any more inhospitable than she'd already observed, but the anxious looks on the women's faces assured her that he could.

"He hires your sister to go up there every couple of weeks and clean the place so it's always ready for occupancy," Gloria said to Pauline, a hopeful expression on her face. "Maybe she would go up and stay with him."

Pauline shook her head. "She can't. Her daughter's baby-sitter has been sick, and June's been having to take care of her grandchildren so her daughter can go to work."

Gloria sighed again. "That leaves one of us."

Watching them, Amanda could see that neither relished the idea of breaching Hawk's lair.

"I've still got a lot of preparing to do for your party," Pauline said quickly.

Gloria turned to Amanda, a plea in her eyes.

It occurred to Amanda that she didn't even know where Hawk's place was. She'd thought this was his home. But she saw the request in Gloria's eyes and knew she couldn't turn her back on a fellow human being who needed help.

"I'll go," she heard herself volunteering grudgingly. In the next moment she was questioning her sanity. Hawk wasn't her problem. If he didn't want people he knew at his place, he certainly wouldn't want her there.

Relief showed on Gloria's face. "You are the most logical choice. I really need to stay here to take care of Juliet, and Pauline does have a lot to do before the party."

"I'll get the food together while you draw her a map," Pauline said, already heading toward the refrigerator.

As Gloria hastily began scribbling directions and Pauline bustled around the kitchen, Amanda had the distinct impression the women wanted to speed her on her way before she could change her mind.

Chapter Four

"This is not a road. It's a trail barely wide enough for a vehicle," Amanda complained as her car bumped along the rutted, narrow access road that cut through Jerome land to Hawk's sanctuary. Hawk had gone, she'd learned, to the home he'd shared with his great-grandfather. When Speckled Owl had died, he'd left all that was his to his great-grandson. And although Hawk had moved into Jack Jerome's home, he'd kept his great-grandfather's place as it was.

"It's my guess he was planning to go back there and live by himself when he turned eighteen," Pauline had told Amanda as they carried the food and supplies out to Amanda's car. "But by then his daddy was training him to run this place. It'd been clear from an early age that Mr. Jason wasn't interested in ranching, and Jack wanted a Jerome, even one born on the wrong side of the blanket, to be in charge. So Hawk continued to stay here, but every once in a while he goes off and spends some time by himself in that cabin. Guess you could say it's his private 'getting away from everything and everyone' place.''

Amanda jerked the wheel to one side to avoid a particularly large rock lying in the path of her car. "And now I'm going to invade that privacy," she muttered unhappily. And Hawk wasn't going to like it—of that she was certain.

Ahead of her, on the crest of a hill, she saw her destination. It was more of a house than a cabin, she decided as she parked in front of the small, one-story structure. She was surprised by how well kept it looked.

Armed with the basket of food, she knocked on the front door.

"Whoever you are, go away!" a voice barked from within.

"How gracious. I'd love to come in," she said sarcastically under her breath. The temptation to enter, deliver the basket of food and leave was strong. And if he's not as sick as we thought he was, that's exactly what I'm going to do, she promised herself as she tried the doorknob. It wasn't locked.

Pushing the door open, she stepped inside. Before taking a second step into Hawk's domain, she paused with the door still open behind her and let her gaze travel around the interior. The room she'd entered was obviously the main living area. A sofa and chairs were grouped in front of a fireplace to her left. To her right and toward the back was the kitchen and dining area. Framed pictures cluttered a table by the couch.

Handwoven rugs hung on the walls. There were no curtains on the windows. The furniture was neither new nor plush, but it was functional. Several rough-hewn pieces looked handmade. There was no touch of feminine softness anywhere. And yet it felt like a home. A man's home. Hawk's home.

"I see Pauline decided to provide me with food, after all."

Amanda's gaze shifted to Hawk seated in one of the chairs by the fireplace. He looked ten times worse than he had when he'd left the house.

"Leave it on the table," he ordered.

Ignoring the dismissal in his voice, Amanda crossed the room, set the basket down and began unpacking it. "You should be in bed," she said curtly.

He'd closed his eyes and leaned his head back. Then he opened them but didn't look at her. He gazed toward the door. "I'll go to bed as soon as I've taken care of my horse."

Amanda doubted he could even stand. He certainly wasn't in any condition to take care of Loco. She drew a terse breath. "I'll take care of the horse. What has to be done?"

This time he did look at her. "He has to be unsaddled and his water trough filled. But he's not going to let you get near him."

"He doesn't have a choice," she shot back, already on her way to the door.

I have to be crazy, she thought as she headed toward the corral where the black stallion was standing, watching her approach. First, she'd volunteered to take care of Hawk. I didn't really have a choice about that, she argued in her defense. And now she was on her way to probably getting maimed by his horse. "I think I read someplace that if you don't show fear, you and the animal should get along just fine," she reasoned aloud. In the next instant it occurred to her that the article might have been referring to dogs.

Reaching the corral, she looked the stallion in the eye. "This has not been the best day of my life," she informed the beast. "And I'm in no mood to do battle with you. You need your saddle removed, and I'm the only one here capable of doing that, so you'd better cooperate."

Loco snorted as if displeased with this turn of events. Still, he stood motionless as she opened the gate and entered.

He looked even larger and stronger than she remembered. She came to a stop beside him. If he did decide to do her harm, he could. "I'm not real good at this," she continued, talking more to calm her own nerves than with any real hope of soothing the animal. "In fact, this is the first time I've ever unsaddled a horse. But it shouldn't require a genius to figure out how to do it. Besides, I've seen a few Westerns in my day and I've watched my cousin saddle a horse." She frowned. "I just wish I'd watched more closely."

As she spoke, she lifted the stirrup and laid it over the saddle. Now she could see the buckle holding the saddle in place. To her relief it came loose fairly easily. Reaching up, she grasped the saddle by the back and the horn and half lifted, half slid it off. The blanket came with it. Picking the heavy cloth up out of the dust, she started to shake it, then abruptly stopped herself. No sense in making any sudden moves that might spook the stallion, she decided, laying the blanket over the saddle and returning her full attention to Loco.

"So far, so good," she murmured, looking at his bridle and wondering how to remove it.

"Start by unfastening the buckle on the side," a male voice ordered curtly.

Amanda jerked around to see Hawk standing on the other side of the corral fence, his knuckles white as he gripped the top rail for support.

Following his instructions, she quickly finished stripping the gear off the stallion. Once free, Loco took a few steps back, then stood watching her.

"You have to pump that handle up and down for water."

Amanda turned to see Hawk looking past her to the small barn that opened into the corral. Following his line of vision, she saw a spigot with a pump handle attached beside a trough to the left of the barn doors. She crossed to the spigot and began to move the handle up and down. She felt pressure building, then water poured into the trough.

When she'd determined that there was enough water for the horse, she went back to where the saddle lay in the dust. Before bending to pick it up, she looked at Hawk. With his darkly suntanned skin, she'd never thought she would see him looking as pale as he did. A shiver of fear for him ran through her. "Is there anything else I need to do?" she asked.

"There's a barrel of feed in the barn. Put some in a bucket and set it out. He can get the hay himself."

She nodded toward the house. "I'm sure I can handle this on my own now. Loco seems to be accepting my presence. You go back inside." Having issued this order, she picked up the saddle and carried it into the barn.

But when she came out a couple of minutes later with the bucket of oats, Hawk was still standing by the fence. Setting the bucket down near the trough, she scowled at him. "I told you to go back inside."

"I needed to rest a minute," he replied gruffly.

Looking at him, the truth dawned on her. "You can't get back to the house on your own." Concern mingled with anger at his stubbornness. "You could have told me that, and I would have helped you before I finished taking care of your horse," she scolded, moving toward him.

"I can make it on my own," he growled.

Amanda paused to refasten the gate of the corral, then turned to see him letting go of the fence. As he took a step, he swayed precariously. Dashing to him, she slipped under his arm, using her body like a crutch.

"I can't believe Loco let you get near him," Hawk mumbled, as she helped him to the house.

"He's smarter than his owner. He knows when he needs help, and he's willing to accept it graciously," she returned dryly.

When Hawk remained silent, Amanda glanced up at him. He looked dazed. Doubt that he could make it all the way to the house caused a rush of fear. He was too large for her to carry. Just keep him moving, she commanded herself silently.

Relief swept through her as they passed through the front door.

Hawk shifted toward the left. "That way," he directed in a voice barely above a whisper.

They entered a small bedroom. A twin-size bed was set against one wall. As they reached it, Hawk slid off her shoulder and into a sitting position on the mattress. "You can go back to the ranch now," he said, then closing his eyes, he fell sideways, his head landing on the pillow while his feet remained on the floor.

Talk about someone determined not to accept help from anyone, she thought. He didn't even have the strength to lift his legs onto his bed, but he was ordering her out of his house.

I can understand why Pauline and Mrs. Jerome didn't want to come up here, she mused as she lifted his legs up onto the bed, then pulled his boots off. When and if he did get better he'd probably bite her head off for staying. But she knew she wasn't going to leave. Whether he liked it or not, he was going to receive her help.

After setting his boots aside, for a long moment she stood looking down at him irresolutely. She knew he'd be more comfortable with his jeans and shirt off. Then her jaw firmed. She drew the line at disrobing the man.

He shivered and she frowned worriedly. There was no way she was going to be able to get him under the covers he was now lying on. There had to be other blankets in the house, she reasoned.

An army-surplus trunk sat against the far wall. Opening it, she stood for a moment looking down at the contents in surprise. The trunk was filled with books by such writers as Jack London, Mark Twain and Winston Churchill.

Glancing over her shoulder to the bed, she wondered if the man lying there had actually read them. Then she saw him shiver again and the question was shoved to the back of her mind. She closed the trunk and opened the closet door. On the shelf she found a blanket, which she took down and spread over him.

Reluctantly she felt his forehead. It was hot and she wondered if she should call a doctor. Instead, she decided to call the ranch. But when she went back into the main room, she discovered there was no phone. Of course he wouldn't have a phone, she fumed inwardly. That would be too civilized.

"Calling a doctor wouldn't do any good, anyway," she informed the emptiness surrounding her. "He'd just tell me to let Hawk sleep, get some aspirin down him if I could and make sure he has fluids."

She went to the kitchen table where she reached into the basket and found the bottle of aspirin. "Back to the lion's den," she ordered herself. Reentering Hawk's room, she woke him and made him swallow two of the tablets. To her relief, he fell immediately back to sleep. She returned to the kitchen. Pauline had sent the recipe and ingredients for chicken soup. Amanda doubted Hawk would feel like eating anytime soon, but too tense to sit, she busied herself cooking.

When the soup was finally simmering, she checked on Hawk. Laying her hand on his forehead, she was certain his fever was down a little. She breathed a sigh of relief. If he'd been any hotter or even the same, she'd promised herself she would find some way to get him to a doctor.

But at least for the moment she would not have to disturb him. Even asleep, he looked grim, and the last thing she wanted to do was wake him. She thought of him in the same category as a sleeping beast. *You've checked on him. Now go back into the living room,* she commanded herself. Instead, she could not resist touching his cheek. She told herself she was merely double-checking his temperature. But it was the tautness of the muscles and the texture of his skin that held her attention.

He issued a low growl and his jaw twitched in a sign of irritation.

Immediately she broke the contact and took a step back. Her heart was beating double time and she felt like a kid who'd just won a dare. The old adage Let Sleeping Dogs Lie flashed into her mind. Good idea, she decided.

Back in the kitchen, she stirred the soup, checked the heat beneath it to make certain it wasn't too high, and again left it to simmer. That done, she considered finding something to read, or simply sitting and relaxing. But a tenseness caused her to wander around the room. It wasn't exactly an uneasiness. It was, she admitted, curiosity.

She'd always prided herself on respecting other people's privacy. And there was certainly no reason for her to be the least bit interested in Hawk Stone. He was the most disagreeable person she'd ever met.

Nevertheless, she found herself approaching the table containing framed pictures. Picking up each in turn, she studied them. A very pretty Native American woman was in a couple of them. In one she was holding a baby and in another she was standing with a young boy at her side. Amanda was sure these were photos of Hawk and his mother. A very old Indian was in another and there were a couple of pictures of Hawk with an elderly Native Americans couple and the same old man. Amanda decided that he was probably Speckled Owl and the others Hawk's grandparents. There were no pictures, she noted, of the Jeromes.

A trickle of perspiration ran down her cheek, bringing her mind back to more practical matters. It was early summer. The morning had been pleasant, but now the sun was causing the house to heat up. Amanda set the last picture aside and began opening windows. In Hawk's room she noticed that he'd kicked the blanket off. Fresh air, she decided, was better than letting the room get stagnant. She opened his window, then spread the cover over him once again. A lock of hair had fallen on his brow. Without thinking, she combed it back with her fingers. The feel of the thick dark strands caused a rush of heat to spread through her. Jerking her hand away, she scowled at herself.

Hawk opened his eyes. "I thought I asked you to leave," he grumbled.

Before she could respond, his eyes had closed again. She doubted he even really knew he'd spoken. "I suppose I shouldn't feel personally insulted by his less than gracious behavior," she muttered as she left the bedroom. "He snaps at everyone indiscriminately."

Well, maybe not everyone, she admitted as she wandered outside. He'd been kind to Juliet. He'd even given his niece that whistle. "He was probably hoping to save himself the inconvenience of another after-dark search," she reasoned, refusing to give him too much credit for goodness.

A tall, lone oak tree stood in the yard. Amanda guessed it had been planted there. The arid terrain didn't seem to encourage the growth of such large trees. Prairie grasses and shrub pines appeared to make up most of the vegetation. A weather-worn rocking chair was shaded by the old oak. Seating herself in it, she let the warmth of the day invade her body. The air smelled of earth, horses and very faintly of prairie roses.

An unexpected tranquillity spread through her. A roughly made three-legged stool sat near the base of the tree. Using her foot, she maneuvered it over in front of her. Then, propping her feet on the stool, she leaned back and closed her eyes.

An image of an Indian began to form in Amanda's mind. She judged him to be in his late twenties, maybe a little older. He was wearing a loincloth, buckskin leggings, a sheathed knife hanging at his hip and moccasins. Above the waist he wore only a distinctive beaded necklace. A leather headband circled his head. Below it, his hair hung long and loose, except for a slender braid on one side decorated with feathers. There was no war paint on his face, but his expression was as grim as a man on his way to battle. He did, in fact, remind her of Hawk. His shoulders were broad and his stomach hard and lean.

Her breathing became deeper and the image more vivid. He stood watching her. She had the impression he wasn't certain if he should welcome her or consider her an intruder. Then he turned and started walking away. Amanda followed. Suddenly a shot rang out.

Amanda jerked awake, kicking over the stool and grabbing the arms of the rocking chair to steady herself. Loco whinnied in protest as a second loud bang reverberated through the air. Now fully awake, Amanda saw a yellow pickup truck pulling up near her car and realized that what she'd thought were shots were merely backfires from that vehicle.

"Sorry about the noise," the driver called out as he climbed down from the cab. "I made the mistake of letting my grandson work on my truck. He did something to give it more power, but now it lets everyone for miles know when it's coming."

The speaker was an Indian. Amanda judged him to be on the downhill side of sixty, but beyond that she couldn't guess. His long white hair was braided into a loose plait that hung down the middle of his back. He wore jeans, a shirt and cowboy boots. A leather thong on which animal teeth had been laced hung around his neck.

Regaining her composure, she rose. "Hello," she said as he approached.

"I'm Walter Bearclaw." He held out his hand.

"Amanda MacGreggor," she replied, accepting the handshake.

Walter nodded, his gaze traveling over her with friendly interest as he released her hand. "We don't see many strangers in these parts."

To her surprise, Amanda found herself immediately liking this man. Normally she was cautious about new acquaintances. "I sort of ended up here by accident."

"So I heard." He gave a shrug as if to say how she'd gotten there was of no importance. "Pauline called to tell me Hawk was sick. She figured he might give you some trouble, so she asked me to drop by."

Relief spread through Amanda. *I knew he was someone I should like*, she told herself. Aloud she said, "You've come to take care of Mr. Stone? I can go back to the ranch?"

Walter grinned. "No. I like Hawk and I want to keep it that way. He's never taken well to being nursed or coddled."

"It's been my experience that he doesn't take anything well," she returned, unable to hide her disappointment.

Walter's grin softened into a sympathetic smile. "I know Hawk can be cantankerous. But he's a good man. Just keep in mind that his bark's worse than his bite." He held out a small bag toward her. "I brought some crushed herbs. Add a tablespoon to a cup of boiling water. Let it simmer for a few minutes, then have Hawk drink it."

"Thanks," she managed to utter politely, accepting the bag. As the man started back to his truck, she considered begging him to stay. But she was sure he wouldn't. Watching him drive away, she shook her head at her naïveté. She was the unlucky newcomer who'd been manipulated into taking the job nobody wanted.

"Of course, once Mr. Hawk Stone is on his way to recovery, I can pack my bags and leave," she reminded herself as she entered the house. "The others all have to stay and put up with him."

"You can pack your bags right now and get out."

Amanda jerked her gaze to the sofa. Hawk was seated there, an expression of grim concentration on his face, as if he had to fight to maintain an upright position. "What are you doing out of bed?" she demanded curtly.

"I thought there was a war going on out there," he growled. "Got as far as here before I saw Walter's truck."

Concern overrode her irritation. "You look like death warmed over. You need to go back to bed." She started toward him, but he held out a hand in a signal for her not to come any closer.

"Go back to the ranch," he ordered.

Amanda's patience snapped. "I'd love to. But unlike wounded, ill or old elephants who are allowed by their herd to go off alone to the fabled elephant graveyard and suffer in solitude, you're going to have to endure my company." Her jaw set with purpose, she headed toward him again. "Now, for both our sakes, you're going back to bed so you can get well and I can get on with my life."

"You're a stubborn, bullheaded woman," he snarled up at her as she reached him.

"I prefer to think of myself as determined," she returned, refusing to let him goad her.

A grin suddenly teased at one corner of his mouth. "My great-grandfather would have liked you."

Amanda's heart skipped a beat. For one brief second he actually looked boyishly mischievous. Then his scowl was back.

"I can manage on my own," he said, pushing himself to his feet.

The rejection in his voice was strong. He couldn't have been clearer about refusing her help if he'd actually ordered her not to touch him. Amanda took a step back to give him room. But when he swayed, she again moved toward him.

Holding on to the arm of the couch, he glared at her. "I came up here so I wouldn't pass this flu on to anyone. Now stay away from me."

She met his glare with impatience. Even if his motives were altruistic, he didn't have to be so disagreeable. "It's too late for me to worry about whether or not I'm going to get sick. However, if you want to be macho about this, go ahead." Stepping back, she waved her arm for him to continue on to the bedroom alone.

His jaw firmed until it was a sharp rigid line. Moving slowly, he made his way back to his bed.

Watching him, Amanda was poised to dash to his aid if he began looking as if he was going to fall. To her relief he didn't.

The man's impossible, she decided as she saw him sink back onto the bed. Then remembering the bag of herbs, she busied herself making the hot drink.

It definitely smelled medicinal, she thought as she stirred the steaming brew. She was sure Hawk would snarl at her and refuse to drink it. But she did need to get some liquid into him or he'd become dehydrated. She grimaced at the cup of herbal brew. She'd use it as a bargaining chip. She'd tell him he either had to drink it or some of the broth from her chicken soup. Because she'd made the soup, he'd probably opt for this stuff! she thought wryly as she headed for his room.

He opened his eyes when she entered. "I'm trying to sleep." His tone held the order for her to get out.

"You have to have some liquid," she replied, refusing to be bullied. "Walter Bearclaw brought some herbs for me to use to make this for you. And you're going to drink it."

For a brief moment, he lay glaring up at the ceiling, then to her surprise he eased himself into a sitting position. "Give it to me."

Stunned that he appeared to be willing to drink the stuff, she approached the bed and handed him the cup.

His nose crinkled. "Walter's a good medicine man, but I wish he'd come up with some better-tasting concoctions," he grumbled as he took a sip. His gaze shifted to her. "You don't have to watch me. I said I'd drink it."

"Good," she replied, and strode out. She didn't stop in the living room but continued outside and sat down in the rocking chair under the tree. He was bound to get well quickly, she reasoned. He was too disagreeable for even a germ to survive prolonged contact.

* * *

It was late afternoon when the sound of an approaching car caught Amanda's attention. Setting aside the book she'd been reading, she rose from the rocking chair. As the vehicle neared, she recognized Gloria Jerome as the driver.

"You look as if things are going well." Gloria's expression was one of relief as she and Juliet joined Amanda in the shade of the tree.

"Well enough," Amanda replied, hoping the woman had come to take over the nursing duties.

"Is Uncle Hawk going to be all right?"

Amanda looked down at Juliet. The little girl was clearly worried. "He'll be fine. He's too irascible to be sick long."

Juliet frowned. "What's irascible?"

"It's the way a great many men are when they're ill," Gloria replied with an encouraging smile at her granddaughter. Then her expression became serious as she returned her attention to Amanda. "I really am sorry you have to be the one to take care of Hawk, but we really have no alternative."

"I know," Amanda conceded, hiding her disappointment as she realized she was not going to be rescued from this duty. A tug on her shirt caused her to glance down.

"What's irascible?" Juliet demanded again.

"Difficult to get along with," Amanda replied.

Juliet grinned with relief. "Uncle Hawk's like that a lot. But he's nice, too." She held her whistle up for Amanda to see. "He gave me this so I won't get lost again. Maybe he'll make one for you."

Amanda smiled. "Maybe." When hell freezes over, she added to herself.

"How is Hawk doing?" Gloria asked, genuine concern in her voice.

"He's sleeping a lot and his fever seems to be going down," Amanda replied.

Gloria looked pleased. "Good. I'm sure you're doing an excellent job." She motioned toward the car. "I brought a few more supplies. Pauline wanted to be sure you had plenty to eat."

Amanda followed Gloria and Juliet back to the vehicle.

Gloria took a large picnic basket out of the back seat and handed it to her. "I really don't want to expose Juliet to the flu," she said with polite apology, "so we'd better be leaving."

A couple of minutes later, Amanda watched the car disappear into the distance. Turning back to the house, she observed dryly, "Hawk certainly has a knack for keeping people at arm's length."

In the darkness, Amanda looked at the luminous dial on her watch. It read two forty-five. It had been her experience that the worst part of any sickness always seemed to occur in the early hours of the morning. Apparently this observation was holding true.

She'd been asleep in the second bedroom which was across the main living area from Hawk's room. From the pictures on the dresser and the clothes still hanging in the closet, she guessed this had been Speckled Owl's sleeping quarters. Not feeling welcome in this house, she'd chosen not to change into the nightgown she'd brought. Instead, she'd remained dressed in her jeans and shirt and simply covered herself with a blanket she'd found in the closet.

Movement from Hawk's side of the house had woken her. Outside, a full moon cast a silvery glow over the prairie. Inside, the moonlight streaming through the windows allowed her to see what she was doing as she left the bed and went to the door of her room. She could hear him in the bathroom throwing up. Uncertain of what would be the best action to take, she stood frozen by indecision.

Hawk came out of the bathroom and went back into his room. She'd thought he hadn't noticed her until he gave the door a hard push causing it to swing shut with a bang.

"Obviously he doesn't want me bothering him," she informed the darkened house. She told herself to go back to bed. Instead, she stood staring at his closed door. She was here to look after him. She couldn't go back to bed until she knew he was all right. Cursing her conscience because she was sure it was going to get her yelled at, she padded across the floor in her bare feet. Reaching his door, she knocked.

There was no answer.

Her rational side was sure he was simply ignoring her. But she couldn't rid herself of the nagging fear that he might be incapable of answering. Drawing a frustrated breath, she opened the door.

His clothes had been discarded haphazardly on the floor. He was lying on his stomach on the bed, a pair of briefs his only covering. The moonlight coming in through the window played over his body. I've seen men in broad daylight striding around in skimpier swimming trunks, she told herself. But they hadn't caused her legs to feel this weak. I wasn't afraid they were going to bite my head off, either, she reasoned, attempting to explain the acute effect seeing him like this was having on her.

Unable to resist, she let her gaze travel along his long form. It looked decidedly sturdy. This is no time to develop an intense interest in the male physique, she scolded herself.

His arm suddenly moved and in the next instant he was covered by a blanket. "Did you come in here for a reason?" he growled, not lifting his head from the pillow.

She heard the edge of self-consciousness in his voice. He was embarrassed that she'd seen him almost naked. That he was shy stunned her. "I wanted to make certain you were all right."

"I'm alive and I feel better," he replied. "Now will you please go away so I can sleep?"

Amanda's gaze narrowed on him. "Are you sure you aren't delirious? You said please."

"I'm in no mood for your sarcasm," he growled back. "Get out."

"Now you sound more normal," she returned and made a quick exit.

On the way back to her bed, Amanda frowned musingly. She'd been sure Hawk never allowed himself to be affected by others. But he'd definitely been embarrassed. She grinned at this surprisingly human side of him. Then her frown returned. He might have a more human side, but those instances when it was exposed were clearly rare and obviously a strain on him.

Leaving her door open so she would hear him if he left his room again, she lay down on the bed and again pulled the blanket over her. A realization suddenly struck her. She knew she wasn't welcome in this house, and yet she felt comfortable and relaxed lying there.

"I'm just tired. Anyplace I could lie down would feel inviting," she assured herself. And closing her eyes, she slept.

Chapter Five

Amanda groaned quietly in protest as she awoke. A soft squeaking sound caused her to open one eye. Hawk's door was being opened. She'd ordered herself to sleep lightly but was shocked that such a small noise would wake her. It seemed that all of her senses were acutely attuned to Hawk Stone.

She saw him making his way to the kitchen area. He'd pulled on his jeans, but nothing more. His image mingled with the vague memories of the dream she'd been having. The Indian with the beaded necklace had been there. She remembered following him over the arid landscape in what seemed like an endless journey.

The sound of running water brought her fully awake. She was supposed to be taking care of Hawk. So get up and see if he needs help, she commanded herself. But, she admitted, she was a little embarrassed to face him this morning. It wasn't like her to stand and stare at a nearly naked man. An unexpected heat raced through her at the memory of his long, muscular form. Wondering if her mind was being adversely affected by the prairie air, she tossed off her blanket and left the bed.

She saw Hawk taking a couple of aspirin as she entered the main room.

"I'm much better today," he said gruffly when he saw her. "You can go back to the ranch," he added, striding past her on his way back to his room.

Amanda regarded his retreating back dryly. "Well, good morning to you, too."

Pausing in the doorway of his room, he glanced back at her impatiently. "I appreciate your coming up here, but I really don't need a baby-sitter." Before she could respond, he entered the room and closed the door.

Amanda looked wistfully at the front door. "I'd like to leave," she murmured. Then, her face screwed up into a resigned grimace as her gaze shifted to his bedroom. "I'll see if his fever is gone. If it is, I'm out of here," she bargained with herself.

Approaching the closed door, she knocked.

There was no response.

For a moment she stood indecisively. She didn't want a recurrence of last night when she'd seen him so exposed. "I'm going to count to ten and then I'm coming in," she announced through the barrier.

Again there was no answer.

Her jaw set with firm resolve, she counted slowly, then opened the door. To her relief, he was covered.

"I apologize for being so disagreeable, but I don't like people around when I'm sick," he said in a low growl. "And I especially don't like being beholden to anyone."

Amanda was tempted to tell him that he'd made that abundantly clear. Instead, she said, "Please don't feel you have to be beholden to me. I'm only here because I had no choice."

He nodded as if that was what he'd expected. "I really am doing fine now. I'm just going to rest for a short while, then I'll saddle Loco and get back to work. There's no reason for you to stick around any longer."

Amanda wanted to believe him. But her conscience wouldn't allow it. "I'll just check your temperature," she said, approaching the bed. She wished she had a thermometer. The thought of touching him made her uneasy. Scowling at her cowardliness, she reached out and placed her hand on his brow. It wasn't as hot as it had been yesterday, but he was still running a slight fever. A curious tingle traveled up her arm, and the urge to comb his hair away from his face simply so she could again feel the coarse strands between her fingers was strong. Shaken by this irrational desire, she quickly broke the contact. "You still have a slight fever," she announced in businesslike tones.

Instructions on how he should take care of himself followed by a hasty goodbye were on the tip of her tongue. But when she opened her mouth to speak, she heard herself saying, "You have to stay in bed until the fever is completely gone. Otherwise you risk a relapse. And I'm going to stay and make certain you follow my instructions." Shocked by this declaration, she regarded him grimly. "Besides, I made some chicken soup from scratch and I'm going to make sure you eat it."

His eyes had been closed, now he opened them. "You'll need to feed Loco, too."

Amanda stared at him, amazed that he wasn't giving her an argument.

"You're right about the relapse," he said in answer to the expression of shock on her face.

"Of course I am," she managed to choke out, backing away from the bed. Reaching the main room, she admitted to herself that his being reasonable unnerved her more than his being disagreeable.

Grateful for an excuse to escape, she went out to the corral. "This is just the same as yesterday," she informed the horse as she entered the enclosure. "Either you let me take care of you or you go hungry and thirsty."

He snorted then backed away from her as if to say he wasn't happy about her being there, but since it was necessary he'd accept it.

"Clearly, you and your master are cut from the same cloth," she said as she pumped more water. Loco snorted as if confirming this statement, and she glanced at him over her shoulder. "What's your story? Were you owned by some cruel rancher who beat you?"

"He simply didn't like being tamed. So we came to an agreement. He lets me ride him and I take care of him."

Amanda jerked around to discover Hawk on the other side of the corral fence. "You're supposed to be in bed."

"I wanted to make certain Loco doesn't live up to his name."

She noted that although he was holding on to the fence, he didn't look as if he needed the support. Obviously he was feeling better, but she didn't want him having a relapse that would lengthen her stay here.

"Well, he hasn't," she said. "So you can go right back to the house and back to bed."

A hint of amusement flickered in his eyes. Then it was gone. "I'll just wait until you're on this side of the fence."

Amanda told herself he was probably more worried about his horse than her. Still, his professed concern for her safety taunted her as she got fresh oats for Loco. Even more disconcerting, she'd caught the hint of laughter in his eyes at her bossiness. In that instant, he'd actually looked appealing. He's got the personality of a rattlesnake, she reminded herself as she finished her chores and left the corral.

After securely fastening the gate, she turned to Hawk. Loco had approached him. There was a real tenderness on the rancher's face as he gave the horse a pat on the neck, and the sight caused Amanda's heart to skip a beat. Then he turned to her and his usual grim expression spread over his features.

"I can make it back to the house on my own this time," he said, his tone warning her to keep her distance.

Remaining about four paces behind, she followed him to the house. As they walked, her ire toward him grew. She told herself that his attitude was none of her business. She would be leaving soon and never coming back. Still, his insular air grated on her nerves.

As they entered the house, her patience snapped. "I'll admit you had a difficult childhood, but a lot of people have difficult childhoods and they didn't grow into bitter adults. Don't you think it's time you put the past behind you?"

The moment the words were out, she wished she'd swallowed them. She'd spoken to his back. She saw his shoulders square and braced herself for a sharp retort. But when Hawk turned to her, his expression was shuttered.

In a voice devoid of emotion he said, "My childhood wasn't all that bad. My mother loved me. My grandfather took good care of me. My father even claimed me and made me one of his heirs. And I'm not bitter. I merely prefer to stand alone."

"Well, you've certainly managed to assure that you'll do that," she replied dryly.

A sudden challenge flickered in his eyes. "It would seem that I'm not the only one in this room who has chosen to stand alone."

She frowned at him. "I'm not standing alone. I have a family I care for. Like I told all of you, I'm merely on a quest."

He regarded her narrowly. "You weren't specific about the object of your quest."

"I'm not exactly sure what I'm looking for...."

"But you'll know when you find it," he finished for her.

"Of course."

A tiredness had crept into his features. Turning away from her, he entered his room and lay down.

Amanda went to the refrigerator, took out the soup she'd made yesterday and put it on the stove to heat. She'd sounded confident when she'd confirmed to Hawk that she'd know the object of her quest when she found it, but the truth was, she wasn't even certain there was anything for her to find. Again she questioned the sensibleness of her trek. A restlessness she couldn't quell had sent her on it. But she hadn't expected to find herself nursing a hostile cowboy on a desolate South Dakota prairie.

"It's been my observation that people with caring families, a job and a conservative nature don't go off on unorthodox wanderings," Hawk said.

Amanda looked up from the book she'd been pretending to read. She was seated across the room from him in an overstuffed chair near the fireplace.

Hawk had slept most of the morning. A few minutes ago he'd come looking for food. He'd refused to eat in bed and was now sitting at the table eating a bowl of soup and studying her from behind a grim mask.

She opened her mouth to tell him that her reasons were none of his concern. But his words were nearly an echo of her own thoughts. "It was the diary," she said. The moment the words were out, she scowled at herself. She couldn't believe she'd mentioned the diary to him. Her parents were the only other people she'd even told of the existence of the ancient leather volume.

Hawk's gaze narrowed on her even more. "Diary?"

Amanda admitted she was having some real doubts about coming on this quest. Her parents had been against it. But she'd reasoned that they simply didn't like the idea of her wandering aimlessly around the country. Maybe if a stranger told her how idiotic her behavior was, she'd be able to rid herself of this need to search for some undefinable something. Then she could go home and get on with her life. And Hawk Stone seemed like the perfect person to tell her she was nuts. He sure wasn't the kind to mince words. Even more important, she didn't care what he thought of her. It wouldn't bother her a bit if he thought she was loony.

"My cousin sent it to me," she elaborated. "Her name's Madaline Darnell. Until recently she lived in a place called Smytheshire in Massachusetts. I was there a couple of times. It seemed like a quiet little town."

A shiver ran along Amanda's spine as she recalled her cousin's close brush with death. But then the lust for power does seem to bring out the worst in people, she reminded herself. In Devin Smythe's case it had sent him over the edge into madness. Luckily for Madaline some of what Devin sought existed within Madaline and Colin Darnell. Their bond had saved Madaline.

And now it's my turn to discover my heritage, Amanda thought, again wondering if there was truly something to discover. "Anyway, my cousin came into possession of the diary there," she continued. "It was written by an ancestor of ours."

Curiosity showed in Hawk's eyes. "And that diary brought you here?"

"Not *here* here." Amanda frowned at her obtuseness. "I guess the best way to describe what happened is to say the diary struck a nerve, which is what sent me on this journey."

"Can I assume this ancestor had a wanderlust, too?" he asked wryly.

"No, she was a druid." Amanda gave a mental gasp when she realized she'd said this aloud. She hadn't meant to be quite so open.

"A druid?" Hawk was studying her now as if questioning whether she was safe to be around. "I was under the impression that the druids died out a long time ago."

Amanda saw the dubious look in his eyes and her shoulders squared with pride. "Apparently not." Then, telling herself again that what Hawk Stone thought of her didn't matter, she continued, "Anyway, after I read the diary, I began to think about my ability to find things—not that it's ever been remarkable or anything. But I've had some unusual experiences. I wondered what I would find if I let my instincts guide me. My curiosity got too strong to resist, so here I am."

Interest mingled with skepticism in his expression. "So you're here. Now what?"

Amanda grimaced sheepishly. As she'd expected, her story did sound ridiculous when she told it, but the telling hadn't brought the desired result. She wasn't ready to go home yet. "I don't know. I guess I'll stay for a few more days to help Mrs. Jerome out with her party and then move on."

Hawk's expression became shuttered. "Then you don't think that whatever you were supposed to find is here?"

"If some sort of inherited instincts are guiding me, I'm pretty sure that the only reason I came this way was to find Juliet," she replied.

Hawk nodded his agreement and returned his attention to his food.

Amanda frowned. She'd been sure he'd make some remark that showed he questioned her sanity. In fact, she'd been counting on his doing just that. But he hadn't. Piqued and confused, she regarded him warily. "I expected you to ridicule me."

Hawk looked up at her. "My mother's people believe inanimate objects have spirits. My great-grandfather believed in prophecies and signs. I figure it's not up to me to tell people what to believe or not believe. I wish you luck in finding whatever you seek."

This was not the Hawk she was used to. Another incongruence struck her. "I thought you said you were suspended from school when you were nine and never went back. But I saw the trunk full of books in your room, and you knew who the druids were." The words were out before she could stop them. Then she decided that fair was fair. She'd told him more about herself than she'd planned.

"My father hired a retired schoolteacher to come up here and tutor me. History was her forte." A grin tilted one corner of his mouth. "Her name was Mrs. Reba

Gray, and she refused to put up with any insubordination. She gave me a choice. I could behave and learn from her, or I'd have to go back to school." The smile disappeared and his expression became shuttered. "I figured it was better all round if I stayed here. I'd heard some of the kids kidding Jason and Jasmine about having an illegitimate brother. I didn't like causing them any grief."

"You're not as insular as you want people to believe," she observed.

Challenge flashed in his eyes. "I also didn't go back because I don't like being confined. Mrs. Gray let me set my own schedule, as long as I completed my studies."

Amanda frowned impatiently. "Talking to you is like trying to pet a porcupine. Every time I think you're going to be pleasant, you suddenly start shooting out needles."

He scowled at her. "I didn't ask for your company."

"So you've made clear a number of times," she snapped back, determinedly returning her attention to her book.

Amanda stood staring out the window, indecision on her face. Hawk was definitely better. He'd slept after he'd eaten the first time. A little while ago he'd gotten up and eaten again, then gone back to bed. She glanced over her shoulder toward his bedroom.

All she had to do was go in there and see if his fever was gone. If it was, she could leave, she told herself. But even as she concentrated on the man beyond the door, her gaze shifted to a table near the couch. There were two drawers in the table, and the one closest to her had been attracting her attention for the past couple of hours. The desire to know what was inside was strong, but her respect for Hawk's privacy wouldn't allow her to look.

She jerked her gaze back to his bedroom door. Go on, she prodded herself and made her legs carry her across the room. At the door, she knocked lightly.

There was no response.

Opening it slowly, she looked at the bed. To her relief he was covered from the waist down and he looked as if he was asleep. Quietly she approached the bed, then reached down and placed her hand on his forehead. His temperature felt normal. She quickly withdrew.

Back in the main room, she again stood irresolutely. He was well enough to be left on his own. She could write him a note telling him she'd gone back to the ranch. "And he'd be glad to find me gone when he gets up again," she murmured, certain this was true.

Still, she hesitated. Her gaze again shifted to the drawer in the table. She jerked her attention back to his bedroom door. "Maybe I should wait until he wakes up the next time, just to be on the safe side," she said resignedly under her breath.

Abruptly the door opened and Hawk emerged. He'd pulled on his jeans and shirt. But he hadn't buttoned the shirt, and she found her attention drawn to the hard musculature of his chest. Quickly she raised her gaze to his face.

"I feel fine, just tired," he said. "I appreciate your coming up here and taking care of me, but I think the time has come for you to go."

Amanda nodded her agreement. The sooner the better, she thought as she went into the other bedroom and gathered her things.

Hawk was sitting in the chair by the fireplace when she came back out. Pausing at the front door, she asked, "Do you have any messages for anyone at the ranch?" she asked.

"Tell them I'll be back tomorrow," he replied.

Amanda again nodded her agreement. But even as her hand reached for the doorknob, her gaze swung back to the drawer in the table.

"Is something wrong?" Hawk asked, a note of impatience in his voice.

"No." That he wanted her gone in a hurry was obvious, but the need to know what was in that drawer was growing stronger by the moment. Her jaw firmed. "Can I look in that drawer?"

Rising from his chair, Hawk approached her. "Which drawer?"

He's going to think I'm incredibly nosy, she was sure. Then she reminded herself that she didn't care what he thought. "The one to the right in that table." She pointed as she spoke.

Hawk crossed to the table and opened the drawer indicated. Stepping back, he motioned for her to take a look.

"I'm not usually this nosy," she said, embarrassed by her forwardness and yet unable to stop herself from pulling the drawer out even more.

The contents were jumbled, obviously tossed in haphazardly. There was a sheathed knife. The leather of the sheath was cracked and worn, and the handle of the knife dark with age. There was also a pocket watch with a fob chain and what looked to be a gold nugget hanging from the chain. And there was a narrow headband with beaded strips of leather hanging down from it. Some documents, yellowed with age, were there, too. An uneasiness spread through her. The knife and headband looked familiar.

Then she remembered studying the photographs of Hawk's family. That was surely where she'd seen them, she decided.

Her hand moved to the papers to shift them aside.

"That's the deed to this land. It wasn't easy for my great-great-grandfather to obtain. But he considered this piece of land sacred and devoted his life to obtaining it."

Amanda had glanced toward Hawk when he spoke. Now she turned her attention back to the drawer. Every muscle tensed. She'd moved the papers to one side. Lying exposed was the beaded necklace the Indian in her dream had worn. She touched it tentatively. "Was this lost?"

"No." Hawk studied her with a shuttered gaze. "It belonged to my great-great-grandfather."

Amanda drew a relieved breath. Obviously she'd seen a picture among those on the table of the Indian who haunted her dreams. He'd just caught the fancy of her subconscious and that was why she was dreaming about him. Her gaze shifted to the photographs. "Which one is he in?" she asked.

"I have no pictures of him."

Her sense of relief vanished. She frowned at the necklace in frustration. "I don't understand."

"What don't you understand?" Hawk demanded.

She looked up to see him studying her with cool interest. "I've had a couple of dreams about your great-great-grandfather," she replied. "At least I suppose it's him. The man I see is wearing this necklace."

Hawk cocked an eyebrow. "And what happens in these dreams?"

She shrugged. "Nothing, really. He walks and I follow. But I have no idea where we're going. He never actually leads me anywhere."

Hawk smiled dryly. "If he should ever lead you somewhere, I'd appreciate your letting me know. If there is a gold mine on this land, he's supposed to know the location. The story is that he was so worried about the white men finding out about the mine and taking it away from him that he only mined small quantities of the gold when he needed funds. Then he'd tell whoever he bartered with that he found the nuggets in a stream. He was supposed to disclose the location of the mine to my great-grandfather, but he died before he ever did."

Hawk's expression became cold. "I figure the mine was played out, but he didn't want to admit it. He wanted to keep the legend of Indian gold alive, so he left the location a mystery to hide the truth." A cynical smile abruptly spread over his face. "And now he's leading you on a wild-goose chase."

"It does seem that way," Amanda agreed. "He certainly hasn't led me anywhere in particular."

A shadow of frustration darkened Hawk's features, then he scowled. "Have you seen enough?"

Again, she was being told it was time for her to go. "Yes, thank you," she replied with calm dignity. She picked up her things from the chair by the door and left.

As she walked to her car, she heard Loco snort. Glancing over her shoulder, she saw the stallion watching her. He whinnied and tossed his head, then took a couple of steps in her direction. It was almost as if he was saying he was sorry to see her go.

Unable to resist the impulse, she dropped her things in the back seat of her car and approached the corral. She had to know if he would let her pet him. But he made no move to come closer to the fence that separated them. "You and your master are definitely cut from the same cloth," she said. "You don't like anyone getting too close, either."

A prickling at the side of her neck caused her to look toward the house. Hawk was standing in the doorway watching her with an expression of impatience. "All right, all right. I'm going," she muttered under her breath, striding back to her car.

"This is one place I'm glad to be getting away from," she added as she climbed in behind the wheel and started the engine.

Later that evening, Amanda sat at the kitchen table with Pauline. The Jeromes had been fed, and now she and the cook were eating a leisurely meal before cleaning up the dishes.

"I suppose Hawk was difficult," Pauline said sympathetically.

"Close to impossible would be a more apt description," Amanda replied.

"Most men aren't easy to get along with when they aren't feeling well," Pauline pointed out philosophically.

Amanda looked at the cook. The woman was clearly trying to make excuses for Hawk. Well, he had so few friends she sure wasn't going to do anything to turn one against him. "I suppose," she conceded.

Pauline's face screwed up into a grimace of concern. "I hope he has enough food. That man can sure eat when he's hungry. And if he hasn't eaten for a couple of days, when he does want food, he's going to be ravenous."

Amanda regarded her wryly. "He'll have the rest of the soup I made. There was a whole chicken cut up in that and most of it's left. There's half the loaf of homemade bread, some of the roast beef, coleslaw and nearly all of the pie you sent me. I doubt he'll starve."

"That should do," Pauline agreed. Uncertainty spread over her features. "I suppose I should warn you before Hawk returns."

Amanda paused in the middle of lifting a spoonful of beef stew to her mouth and looked at the cook. She had the distinct impression she wasn't going to like what the woman told her. "Warn me?"

"Hawk's never felt comfortable eating in the dining room," Pauline said, her words coming out in a rush. "Generally he finds some reason to be either too early or too late to eat with the rest of the family and ends up eating most of his meals in here with me.''

Great! Amanda groaned mentally, as the image of Hawk seated there with them played through her mind. ''Does he just sit here and glower during the meal, or does he talk to you?''

Pauline frowned while Amanda flushed and berated herself for having been so snide.

''I'll admit Hawk's standoffish,'' Pauline said. ''He was that way even as a child. But you have to understand, in a way he's always been the outsider. He's a half-breed to the Sioux and a half-breed to the whites. He's always had to prove himself before he was accepted by anyone. Maybe he just got tired of that. Maybe he decided that the rest of us weren't worth his time. I couldn't blame him if he did.''

''You have a point,'' Amanda admitted, feeling properly chastised. Then her shoulders squared. ''But when someone is being nice to him, he could at least be a little courteous.''

Pauline breathed a sigh. ''Yes, he could,'' she conceded.

Deciding that some other topic was preferable, Amanda considered mentioning the weather. But when she spoke, she heard herself asking, ''Do you and he ever talk?''

''During breakfast he generally tells me about his work schedule for the day so I'll know when to expect him for meals and how to contact him if he's needed at the house.'' A thoughtful expression came over Pauline's face. ''But he never actually talks about himself or what he feels. I do know how much he loves this ranch. That's something he inherited from his father."

"I've gotten the impression all the others want to sell," Amanda said, knowing she was prying but unable to stop herself.

"Jason and Jasmine do. They've never really liked living out here in such a remote area. But I'm not so sure Mrs. Jerome really wants to sell. She knows how much this land meant to her husband. I think she'd be happy if Hawk could buy the place. And I think that if Hawk agreed to sell, she'd allow the sale just to please her children."

Amanda frowned musingly. "But Hawk will never agree to sell, and he can't afford to buy the place."

Pauline nodded in agreement. "That's about it. And as long as he can keep the place running at a profit, Jasmine and Jerome can't do anything."

"It seems that Hawk has chosen a path in life that will keep him an outsider," Amanda observed.

"Seems that way," Pauline confirmed.

Later that night as she lay in bed, Amanda found herself worrying about Hawk having a relapse and being alone. Then she frowned. He was fine, she assured herself. Besides, he'd be happier alone.

Her frown deepened. She could understand why he was the way he was. But that didn't make him any easier to get along with. While she was here, she'd steer a wide path around him.

Chapter Six

Early the next morning, Amanda stood grimacing at her image in the mirror. She'd vowed to keep a distance between herself and Hawk, and yet he'd strode in and out of her dreams all night. "The man's a menace to my sanity," she grumbled.

Wanting to put him out of her mind, she hurried downstairs to help Pauline fix breakfast. But as she entered the kitchen, she came to an abrupt halt and blinked. Like a bane that refused to go away, there was Hawk seated at the table.

Seeing Amanda, Pauline smiled. "Looks like he's got his appetite back," she said with satisfaction as she poured him a cup of coffee.

Hawk turned to Amanda. "Morning," he said.

She'd expected something resembling a growl to come from him. But his greeting had actually been polite. A bit stiff, but polite nonetheless. "Obviously you're still feeling a little under the weather," she remarked. "The hostile edge hasn't returned to your voice."

Pauline looked shocked.

She's not nearly as shocked as I am, Amanda thought, unable to believe she'd just taken a jab at Hawk. This wasn't like her. She was normally reserved and never sought out confrontations. The man brings out the worst in me, she decided. Barely breathing, she waited for his response.

But it was Pauline who spoke first. "Hawk can be real pleasant when he wants to be," she declared, her gaze shifting uneasily from Amanda to Hawk then back to Amanda.

"I can be real unpleasant at times, too." Hawk grinned sheepishly at Pauline. "You've never been shy about telling me so."

Surprise registered on Pauline's face. "I never thought you listened to anything I said. I figured I was just whistling in the wind."

His grin disappeared and his expression became shuttered. "I heard you. I'd have to be deaf not to have."

The cook frowned in frustration. "You might've heard, but you didn't pay me any heed. Obviously you gave Amanda a bad time."

Hawk shrugged. "You know what they say about trying to teach an old dog new tricks."

"In your case, I think trying to befriend a junkyard dog would be a better comparison," Amanda said, then flushed as she again saw shock on Pauline's face. Hawk turned and cocked an eyebrow, as if to say he thought she'd gone a bit too far with this analogy. "I apologize," she said quickly, adding honestly, "I really don't know what's come over me. I'm not usually this impolite."

A smile played at the corners of Hawk's mouth. "Be careful. People are going to start thinking you've spent too much time in my company and my bad manners are rubbing off on you."

Amanda couldn't believe it. He was laughing at himself. Even more disconcerting, that smile actually made him look appealing. My mind really is going, she chided herself, amazed that she could have used the word "appealing" a second time in thinking of Hawk Stone. Aloud she said, "Maybe so."

Pauline studied them thoughtfully. "It seems like the two of you have found your common ground."

"So it would seem," Hawk replied, rising from the table.

Feels more like quicksand than ground to me, Amanda thought, but kept this to herself.

As Hawk moved in her direction, Amanda stepped away from the door to give him room to pass. But he didn't continue on out of the kitchen as she thought he would. Instead, he stopped in front of her. His expression, as usual, was shuttered as he faced her.

"I want to apologize for my behavior the past couple of days. I know I was difficult. You treated me better than I deserved. And your soup was good." Reaching into the pocket of his shirt, he pulled out the beaded necklace she'd seen in the drawer. "I want you to have this as my way of apologizing and saying thank-you." As he spoke, he lifted her hand and laid the necklace in it.

His touch sent a current of heat racing through her. Never had she felt such a strong hand, she thought. But then she'd never met such a hard man, she added as she looked up into his cool, gray-green eyes. "This really isn't necessary," she said, uneasy about accepting the gift. After all, this was part of Hawk's heritage. "This necklace must have great sentimental value for you. There's no reason for you to feel you should give it to me."

"It held great sentimental value for my great-grandfather. To me it is merely a string of beads," he replied. Then turning away, he strode to the back door and out of the kitchen.

Amanda looked down at the necklace in her hand. It was another bit of proof that Hawk was a man who was determined not to allow anyone or anything to mean too much to him. She even doubted that this ranch meant as much to him as Pauline thought it did.

"Hawk lied. I've never known him to lie. But he did," Pauline declared.

Amanda's attention shifted to the cook. Pauline was staring at the back door with a perplexed expression on her face. "What did he lie about?" she prodded when it became obvious the cook was going to remain silent.

As if just remembering there was someone else in the room, Pauline turned to her. "That necklace. He lied about its not having any sentimental value to him. After his grandfather died and he came to live here, that necklace was one of the few personal things he brought with him, other than his clothes. Speckled Owl's house and land had been willed to him, and he left most of his belongings there. Like I said before, it was as if he saw coming here as merely a temporary arrangement. It's my guess that if things hadn't worked out the way they did—Hawk's being Jack's choice to run the ranch and all—Hawk would have gone back to his own property the day he turned eighteen.''

Amanda was sure the woman was right about Hawk's not thinking of this house as his home. But she didn't want the conversation to drift in that direction. "So you think he's really attached to the necklace," she said.

"I know he is. He used to keep it on his dresser. One day Jasmine 'borrowed' it without asking. When Hawk discovered it missing, he tore up his room looking for it. Mrs. Jerome threw a fit when she saw the mess he'd made and insisted on knowing what he was looking for. When he told her, she said that Jasmine had said Hawk had given her permission to wear the necklace to school. Hawk looked Mrs. Jerome in the eye and said, 'That necklace belonged to my ancestors. It's mine and I don't want anyone touching it.' He was barely fifteen at the time, but no adult could have been cooler or firmer. I know he intimidated Mrs. Jerome. She got in her car, drove to the school, got the necklace and brought it home." Pauline frowned thoughtfully. "Fact is, I don't think I've seen it since that day until now."

"He had it up at the house Speckled Owl left him," Amanda said in answer to the question in Pauline's voice.

An expression of understanding spread over Pauline's face. "Yes. He would keep anything he considered valuable there."

Amanda studied the necklace in her hand. It didn't make any sense for Hawk to give her something he considered so valuable. They were barely on speaking terms. Then, like a light bulb suddenly switched on, a possible explanation for his gift dawned on her. "I'll be back in a few minutes," she said, and headed out the door after Hawk.

She found him down by one of the corrals with a couple of the wranglers. He saw her coming and sent the men on their way.

"I have a suspicion as to the real reason you gave me this necklace," she said, extending the hand in which she was still carrying the piece of beadwork.

He cocked an eyebrow as if to suggest she was being unfair in accusing him of an ulterior motive. "I gave it to you as a thank-you."

She scowled at him, her expression calling him a liar. "You're hoping that my possessing it will act as a catalyst and help me find your gold mine—like the conjurer who holds on to an article of jewelry from someone in the audience, then tells that person things about themselves."

For a moment he looked as if he was going to deny this, then he shrugged. "I guess that thought did cross my mind. But I was thinking more in terms of the bloodhound who uses the lingering scent on an object to lead him to what he seeks.''

''Now that's a real flattering comparison,'' she returned snappishly, piqued by the less than complimentary image of herself this created.

He drew a harsh breath. ''I don't expect you to understand, but this ranch is as much a part of me as an arm or a leg.''

The depth of emotion she saw in his eyes stunned her. Even more disconcerting, the thought of his losing this ranch caused an intense wave of sorrow to sweep through her. ''I do understand how you feel,'' she said, shaken by this unexpected empathy.

For a brief moment, he looked self-conscious, and she knew he was embarrassed to have been so open about his feelings. Then the cool mask he used to hide his emotions returned. ''As I've already told you,'' he said stiffly, ''if there is a mine, I'm pretty sure it's played out. But if you should get an idea where it might be, I'd appreciate your letting me know.''

''I will,'' she promised.

He nodded and turned to walk away.

''Wait.'' The moment this command was out, she regretted it. The sudden notion she'd had would probably prove futile. She should have experimented in private. But he was already looking at her questioningly. ''I might as well give this a try right now,'' she said.

As he stood watching her, she closed her eyes and concentrated on the necklace in her hand. Because she'd never been able to control her talent before, she honestly expected nothing but blankness. Instead, a vision began to form in her mind. The old Sioux, the one she'd seen in the photographs at Hawk's house, was there. He was lying on his bed. He looked asleep, but she knew he was dead. Standing beside the bed was a boy in his early teens. Grief was etched into his features and tears were rolling down his cheeks. She could see he was trying to cry silently, and the effort was causing his whole body to shake. Dangling from his hand was the necklace she was holding. And she knew without any doubt that the old man was Speckled Owl and the young boy was Hawk. A lump formed in her throat. Unable to bear the scene any longer, she opened her eyes.

"What did you see?"

She looked up to find Hawk studying her narrowly. Unable to bring herself to mention an event she was sure he would rather not be reminded of, she said, "Nothing." She'd expected at least a momentary disappointment to show on his face, but his expression remained cool and emotionless. The man, she marveled, was an expert at covering his feelings.

He nodded his acceptance of her answer. "Thanks for trying."

Amanda extended the necklace toward him. "You can have this back."

He shook his head. "A gift once given cannot be taken back. It's yours."

As he turned and walked away, the image she'd seen haunted her. She'd never had an experience like that before. She'd held hundreds of objects, and they'd never conjured up visions of previous events. She gave herself a shake. Reality check! she ordered. The image was merely due to an overactive imagination. At Hawk's house, she'd seen pictures of Hawk and his great-grandfather. She knew that Speckled Owl was one of the very few people Hawk had cared for. Her imagination had merely combined these facts.

"Considering his ability to show no disappointment when I couldn't locate his gold mine, he probably never even cried openly when his great-grandfather died," she murmured to herself. Still, even if what she'd seen was a figment of her imagination, every instinct told her that the necklace she was holding meant a great deal to the insular cowboy. When she left the ranch, she'd find a way to return it to him.

Amanda smiled as the warm breeze stirred her hair. It was Sunday afternoon. She'd been at the ranch a week. She'd helped with breakfast and, after church, served Sunday dinner. Now she had the rest of the day off, and she'd chosen to go horseback riding in the hills.

Earlier in the week, she'd been invited by Mrs. Jerome to join her and Juliet for their daily ride. Amanda had said she would love to but explained that she'd only ridden a couple of times as a young girl and wasn't skilled. Gloria Jerome had offered instructions and Amanda had learned quickly. In fact, to her surprise, she'd felt totally comfortable in the saddle. After their first ride, Mrs. Jerome had proclaimed her a natural. Since that day, Amanda had gone riding whenever she was invited and today she'd sought permission to go riding on her own.

A prickling on the back of her neck caused her to glance over her shoulder. She was not surprised to see Hawk on Loco in the distance. It seemed as though every time she turned around he was there.

The first day she'd gone riding with Mrs. Jerome and Juliet, she'd looked toward a crest of a hill and seen him. The second time the three had gone out, he'd joined them about forty minutes into their ride. He'd said he'd been out inspecting fences. But Amanda had seen the surprise on Gloria's face when Hawk had continued to ride with them.

Now here he was again. Reining her horse in, she waited for him to join her.

"Afternoon," he said in his usual cool, distant manner as he reached her.

Amanda leveled her gaze on him. "If I was the suspicious type, I'd begin to think you're following me."

A flash of impatience showed in his eyes. "I am."

Amanda stared at him. She couldn't believe he'd admitted it.

"I saw you leaving the ranch alone," he continued. "I didn't think it was wise to let you go out on your own. You're a novice here. Besides, I saw bobcat tracks the other day."

His reasoning, she conceded, sounded rational but then so had all of his other excuses. Challenge showed on her face. "I don't mean just today. Every time I turn around you're there."

He cocked an eyebrow as if he thought she had an overly inflated perception of her charms.

An embarrassed flush began to spread from her neck upward. "I know you're not interested in me as a woman," she snapped. To her consternation, this statement brought a sharp sense of regret. Furious with herself for this irrational reaction, she continued tersely, "So I can only assume you think I might lead you to your gold mine. If that's the case, I've already assured you that I'll tell you if I find it. You don't have to keep dogging my trail."

For a brief moment, he looked as if he was going to deny this accusation, then his expression darkened with suspicion. "I know you saw something when you were concentrating on the necklace a few days ago. There was a marked change of expression on your face."

Amanda wasn't surprised to hear this. Even now the image of the grief-stricken boy was vivid in her mind. She also couldn't fault Hawk for following her. He had only her word that she could be trusted. "I should have told you the truth in the first place," she said. "It would have saved you from wasting your time." But even as the words formed in her mind, she hesitated. She could almost feel the child's pain.

"And what is the truth?" he demanded.

She looked into his icy, gray-green eyes. Again she told herself that her vision was most likely nothing more than romantic fiction. Even if it wasn't, the child who had suffered such grief had grown into a man she guessed would probably feel nothing now. "I saw an elderly Indian. He was in some of the photographs I saw at your place. I assume it was Speckled Owl."

Hawk nodded. "He was in several."

"He was lying on a bed—the bed I used when I was there."

Again Hawk nodded. "That was his room."

Amanda drew a shaky breath. This memory might be easy for him to relive, but it was very difficult for her. "He was dead."

"He chose to die in his own bed," Hawk confirmed tersely.

"There was a young boy standing beside the bed holding the necklace and weeping. I assumed it was you," she finished, choking back the lump that had formed again in her throat.

Hawk's jaw twitched in an obvious struggle to maintain his cool, indifferent expression. "It was," he admitted through clenched teeth.

Amanda saw the same grief-stricken pain in his eyes she'd seen in those of the child. She wasn't sure what shook her most—his sorrow or the fact that she'd actually had a vision of something that had really occurred. Both were unnerving.

"I'm sorry about your great-grandfather," she said, feeling the need to say something consoling.

Hawk's mask was again in place. "He was old. He'd lived a long life. He was ready to go," he said in clipped tones.

Amanda knew by his withdrawal that he didn't want to talk about Speckled Owl. She told herself to drop the subject but instead heard herself saying, "It must have been difficult to lose him."

"People can't live forever." Hawk's gaze shifted to the horizon. "The land is the only thing a person can count on always being there."

"Sort of like a massive security blanket," she mused, then flushed at her analogy. Even adults

needed someone or something to cling to. To insinu-
ate that his love for this ranch was adolescent wasn't
fair. She couldn't blame him if he growled at her, and
she braced herself for a hostile rebuff.

"I guess you could describe it that way," he replied.

Again Amanda found herself staring at him in
stunned silence. Hawk Stone was a very difficult man
to predict.

He motioned in the direction she'd been riding.
"Shall we continue? You lead the way. I'm merely
along as an escort."

She scowled at him impatiently. "Really, you don't
have to accompany me. You can trust me. I've given
you my word I'll tell you if I find your mine."

He met her gaze levelly. "Trusting people doesn't
come easily for me. Besides, I wasn't joking about the
bobcat."

At least he was honest, Amanda thought. "Suit
yourself," she replied, and gave her horse a nudge.

As they started off again, Hawk rode a little way
behind her. Almost immediately, Amanda began to
feel an uncomfortable twinge between her shoulder
blades. He's probably not even looking at me, she
chided herself. Still, just knowing he was back there
made her edgy. Glancing over her shoulder, she said,
"You take the lead. You know this land better than I
do."

Without any further coaxing, he picked up his pace
and passed her. He rode a little ahead and to one side,
giving her a view of his back and little of his profile.
At first she tried to concentrate on the scenery and

then the ground in front of her. But her eyes kept shifting back to him. She found herself recalling that first night they'd encountered each other. She experienced a curious curling sensation in the pit of her stomach when she remembered riding with her arms around him. His body had felt like tensile steel. Her gaze traveled down his long form. His worn jeans fit snug around his thighs, and she found herself wondering if his legs would feel as solidly muscular as his back. She was sure they would. Still, the urge to touch them just to test this assumption was strong.

Abruptly she jerked her gaze away from him. She couldn't believe the paths her mind was taking. These wanton thoughts weren't like her at all. Not that she didn't appreciate a nice male body, but she usually didn't pay quite so much attention or want quite so close a look.

Catching a movement out of the corner of her eye, she glanced to her side and saw that Hawk had slowed enough to take a position beside her. About six feet separated them. "This is your ride," he said. "Figured you should have the privilege of choosing the direction."

She could have sworn there was an edge of discomfort in his voice, as if he'd known she'd been studying him and hadn't liked it. Her own nerves were near the breaking point. Hawk Stone was definitely not the companion she would have chosen as company for a relaxing afternoon.

"Actually, I think it's time to go back," she replied. "I'm not familiar with the land any farther than this."

As she turned her horse, she wondered if he'd try to encourage her to continue, hoping some instinct might lead her to the mine. It was now obvious that even though he didn't hold much hope the mine would provide the solution to his dilemma, he still held at least a shred of belief the legend might be true.

But Hawk said nothing as they started back. Studying him covertly, she was sure she caught a glimpse of relief on his face. Her jaw firmed. He might want the gold, but he didn't like being in her company for any length of time. Well, she wasn't all that pleased with his company, either, she assured herself.

Back at the ranch, at his insistence, she left him to take care of the horses and went up to the house.

She was passing through the hall on her way to the stairs when Jason came out of his study. "Something going on between you and Hawk?" he asked with a playful smile.

He was hinting at some sort of romantic involvement, she was sure. "No, nothing," she replied, thinking how horrified Hawk would be if he knew anyone was even considering this possibility.

"I've noticed he's been keeping a close eye on you," Jason persisted. "And I could have sworn I just saw the two of you ride in together."

The urge to tell him to mind his own business was strong. Then she realized she was overreacting. Jason was merely showing a bit of friendly curiosity. She'd never minded that before. Besides, it would be best to treat this with humor, she cautioned herself. If she snapped at him, he might think she was trying to hide tender feelings for Hawk.

"You're obviously an observant lawyer," she said. "But you've reached the wrong conclusion. He's only interested in the possibility that I might find his legendary gold mine. As for me, I don't think I've ever met such a disagreeable man."

Jason was studying her with interest now. "Any chance you could help him find that mine?"

Clearly he wanted Hawk to have a way to purchase the ranch, and for all their sakes, Amanda wished she could help. But that didn't seem likely. "I don't know. As I've said before, I don't have any control over my ability to find things. Either it happens or it doesn't happen, and since it hasn't happened yet, I doubt it will."

"Well, I for one am glad to simply have your company." Jason's smile warmed. "I was thinking of going into town for a bite to eat and a movie. How about joining me?"

A refusal formed in her mind, then she heard boot-steps behind her. Without even looking, she knew it was Hawk. The need to prove she was considered desirable company by some men overwhelmed her. "I'd love to," she said. "Just give me a few minutes to shower and change."

"Wonderful," Jason replied.

Amanda smiled back, then continued on to the stairs without glancing over her shoulder. Behind her, she heard Jason bidding Hawk a good afternoon and Hawk replying in his usual indifferent tone. What she did and who she did it with were of no interest to Hawk Stone, she pointed out to herself, furious for allowing his presence to goad her into agreeing to a date she didn't really want to go on. However, she'd accepted, and good manners demanded she go through with it. Resigned to her fate, she picked up her pace as Hawk continued down the hall behind her. The more distance she kept between herself and the cowboy, the better.

But upstairs, as she showered, she had serious second thoughts about the date with Jason. She didn't want to encourage his attention, and going out with him would do just that. Accepting the date had been foolish. Following through with it would be even more foolish, she reasoned. There had to be a polite way out of this situation, and she realized with relief that there was.

Instead of putting on the dress she'd worn to church, she chose a pair of khaki slacks and a pastel, summer-weight knit top. Then she gave her hair a quick brushing, tied it back with a scarf, applied just a touch of lipstick, slipped into her sneakers and went in search of Jason. She found him in his study.

"You look terrific," he said with his usual charming smile. Removing his suit coat, he tossed it onto a chair, then began unfastening his tie. "A casual evening was what I really wanted."

Amanda fought not to frown. She'd been sure when he saw her in slacks, he'd be relieved to call off their date. She'd never known Jason to leave the house in anything other than a suit. As a rule, he even wore one when he was at home, and she didn't think she'd ever seen him without a tie. Early on, she'd learned from Pauline that he hated riding and nearly everything else about ranching except for the legalities. His only concession to the rural Western culture in which he lived was his Stetson and cowboy boots. As for these accessories, Amanda guessed they were more affectation than a true display of his taste. Wearing them placed him in "the good ol' boys" club, an asset to any lawyer practicing in these parts.

"I've been thinking that it's really not appropriate for us to go out," she said. "After all, you're my boss."

"My mother is your boss," he corrected. "This house is her domain."

"I still don't feel comfortable about our having a date," she insisted. "I'm very flattered that you asked me. But now that I've had time to think about it, I've concluded that it isn't a good idea. This house might be your mother's domain, but I still think of you as one of my employers."

A sarcastic expression abruptly spread over his face. "If you're saving yourself for Hawk, you'd better not plan on anything permanent. This ranch is all he cares about."

Amanda was startled by this reaction. She'd expected Jason to amicably accept her excuse for not being able to go out with him. After all, it was reasonable. She'd never seen this side of him. There was something that verged on hatred when he said Hawk's name. A theory as to the real reason he'd asked her out occurred to her.

"I'm not saving myself for Hawk," she stated curtly.

Immediately Jason looked repentant. "I'm sorry. I guess my ego doesn't take rejection well."

Amanda had never liked being used, and she refused to allow him to think he could fool her. "I'd be flattered if I thought you had an honest interest in me and that was the real reason your ego feels damaged," she returned, studying him levelly. "But I have a feeling you only asked me out because you thought you were competing with Hawk."

He smiled as if to say this was a ridiculous notion. "You shouldn't put yourself down like that. You're a good-looking woman." Approaching her, he held out his hand. "I hope we're still friends."

His persuasive charm had returned, and when he declared her a good-looking woman there was just the right gleam of admiration in his eyes to give validity to his words. But Amanda was sure this was all an act. Every instinct told her she'd been right in her accusation regarding his real reason for asking her out. He went to the top of her list of people to be wary of. However, she saw no need to encourage animosity between her and Jason.

"Sure," she said, accepting the handshake while silently vowing to keep her distance from him in the future.

As she left the room, she noticed him refastening his tie.

Hunger caused her to head to the kitchen. But as she entered, she wished she'd driven into town by herself. Hawk was seated at the kitchen table with Pauline.

Ignoring him, she smiled a hello at Pauline, then strode over to the refrigerator and took out the leftover roast beef.

"Thought you had a dinner date with my brother."

Amanda looked over her shoulder to see Hawk regarding her with a detached air. Obviously, the question had been born of simple curiosity. His tone and his manner clearly implied he didn't care whether she dated Jason or not. She felt a sharp jab of irritation. The realization that she'd hoped to see even a modicum of jealousy in his eyes rattled her. The man had her thinking totally confused and traveling absolutely irrational paths, she admonished herself. "I decided it wasn't prudent to socialize with one of my employers," she said with matching indifference.

"That's probably a good idea," he conceded, then returned his attention to eating the sandwich on the plate in front of him.

Amanda saw the cook looking questioningly from her to Hawk and back again. To her relief, Pauline said nothing.

Quickly Amanda made herself a sandwich and poured a glass of ice tea. Then she announced, "It's such a pleasant evening I'm going to go eat on the patio," and left. Outside, she drew in a breath of the fresh air and ordered Hawk Stone out of her mind.

For a long while after finishing her sandwich she continued to sit outside. Grudgingly she admitted this wasn't because she was finding the night air relaxing. She was waiting for Hawk to leave the kitchen before taking her dishes back inside. Coward! she chided herself silently. Still, she didn't budge until she saw him heading in the direction of the corrals. Entering the kitchen, she was furious with herself for letting him make her uneasy, but she couldn't deny that he had that effect on her.

"Nice evening," she said to Pauline as she crossed to the sink and began washing her dishes.

"Do you want to talk about whatever is going on between you and Hawk?"

Amanda looked over her shoulder to see the cook studying her narrowly. "There's nothing going on between us," she replied, her tone implying this was the silliest thing she'd ever heard.

Pauline harrumphed impatiently. "He didn't eat any dessert. He always has a piece of my cherry pie, sometimes two at one sitting," she said, as if his apparent lack of appetite gave proof to her assumption that something was amiss.

"Maybe he just wasn't hungry," Amanda returned, sure that nothing she had done could have caused the insular cowboy to change his usual pattern of behavior.

"Whenever Mr. Jason gets the idea that Hawk is interested in something, he goes after it," Pauline persisted.

Amanda turned to look at her. The cook was clearly implying that she thought a romantic triangle was developing. Amanda told herself the notion that Hawk might actually care for her was absurd. But even so, the thought that he might caused a rush of excitement.

"Did Hawk say something to you to lead you to believe he has feelings for me?" she asked bluntly.

Pauline shook her head. "No." Her mouth formed a defensive pout. "But I can sense that something is going on."

Amanda experienced a rush of disappointment, which was immediately followed by self-directed anger. Hawk was an impossible person to get along with, she reminded herself. He was the last man on earth she should want to become romantically involved with.

"The only thing that is going on is that Hawk is hoping I can lead him to his mine," she insisted. "Because of that, he's been keeping a close eye on me. Like you, Jason mistook the reason for Hawk's interest in me and made a play for me. But now that we all understand what's going on, I hope we can get back to business as usual."

Pauline sighed. "The truth is, I keep hoping Hawk will find someone to care for. If he ever does, she'd be one lucky woman. When he makes a commitment, he makes it for life, and when he cares for something or someone, he cares with all his heart."

"You," Amanda said, "are an incurable romantic." But even as she gently chided Pauline, she was forced to admit the cook was right. Hawk was a man who would care deeply. But she also knew his only interest in her was due to the hope that she could help him gain ownership of this ranch. If he wasn't desperate, he would never even give her presence a moment's notice. Not wanting to discuss Hawk any further, she bid Pauline a quick good-night and went up to her room.

Chapter Seven

Amanda stood to one side of the living-room window gazing out at the back patio. It was midafternoon. The day was sunny and the warm breeze stirring the curtains was sweet with the smell of early summer. Hawk was seated on a patio chair, leaning back with his feet propped up on another chair, whittling. Juliet was having a tea party with her dolls at a nearby table.

Amanda had been dusting when she'd first noticed the man and little girl. She'd told herself to ignore them and get on with her work, but instead, she found herself moving to a table even closer to the window. At first, she watched covertly, keeping at least half of her attention on her dusting. But now she was giving the pair outside her full attention.

She'd noticed that ever since Hawk had given the little girl the whistle, Juliet seemed to seek out his company more and more. Their relationship was still rather standoffish, though. Juliet rarely got too near Hawk. And until this moment, Amanda had been sure that although Juliet found her uncle interesting, she remained a little intimidated by him.

However, watching Juliet now, Amanda wasn't certain if the child had actually been intimidated by Hawk and it had taken her this long to work up her courage to approach him, or if she had been merely respecting his desire to be left alone. Whatever the case, the child's behavior toward her uncle was now taking a step in a new direction. While Amanda watched, the little girl poured tea into one of her tiny cups. Then rising from the table, she carried it to Hawk.

"Pauline's making cherry tarts and she said I was to offer you some," she said as she extended the cup of tea toward him. "But this is a tea party, so you have to have tea, too."

Amanda felt a wave of dizziness and realized she'd been holding her breath waiting for Hawk's reaction. Juliet, on the other hand, did not look the least bit anxious. The little girl was regarding the man with a stern expression that dared him to disobey her.

Hawk suddenly laughed. Then, still smiling, he accepted the tiny cup. "Thank you," he said with exaggerated politeness.

"You're welcome," Juliet returned primly, then walked back to the table.

Amanda admonished herself for eavesdropping, but nonetheless, she remained transfixed. She'd never heard Hawk laugh. She'd begun to think he was in-

capable of it. Even more, it had been a really nice
laugh. It seemed to her that he hadn't laughed at the
child but at himself, as if he realized he was taking life
too seriously. And the smile on his face had been gen-
uinely friendly.

"You have to take a sip before you can have a tart,"
Juliet instructed, watching him from her seat at the
table.

Hawk nodded and lifted the tiny cup to his lips.

Amanda couldn't believe her eyes. Hawk Stone was
willingly participating in a tea party!

"Don't get any of those wood shavings in your tea,"
Juliet warned in her best mother's voice as he put
down the cup and resumed whittling.

"Yes, ma'am," Hawk replied, carefully shifting the
direction of his whittling.

"Looks like you're making another whistle," Juliet observed. She turned to one of her dolls, and lifting her own whistle, showed it to the toy. "Hawk
made this for me. Isn't it clever?" Then turning back
to Hawk, she said, "Lillie thinks your whistle is
clever."

He turned and tipped his hat toward the table.
"That's very kind of Lillie to say."

"She's a very kind doll," Juliet replied. "Now,
Harriet—" she paused to point to another doll seated
across the table "—she can be a real bitch."

Amanda saw Hawk's jaw twitch as he fought not to
laugh out loud.

"Juliet, I'm sure your grandmother wouldn't want
you using language like that," Pauline admonished as
she came out of the kitchen carrying a plate of tarts.

Juliet met this scolding with a pout. "I'm not talking to Nana. I'm talking to Hawk."

"It doesn't matter who you're talking to," Pauline said, setting the tray on the table. "You should always be ladylike and polite."

Juliet pursed her lips even more, then said, "Hawk isn't always polite, and no one tells him he has to be."

Pauline looked at a loss for words.

"That's because they know I'm irreformable," Hawk said in an easy drawl.

Juliet stared at him in puzzlement. "What's irreformable?"

"It's a man who hasn't met the right woman yet," Pauline interjected pointedly.

Hawk's expression became serious as his gaze leveled on Pauline. "No woman would want the kind of life I could give her."

"You can't know that for sure, and you're never going to find out with that attitude," Pauline snapped. Shaking her head at his stubbornness, she set the tray of tarts on the table and stalked back into the kitchen.

"What kind of life could you give her?" Juliet asked.

Hawk's attention jerked to the child, giving Amanda the impression he'd forgotten she was there. "A very difficult one," he replied, easing himself out of the chair.

Approaching the table, he sat the small teacup down. "Thanks for the drink."

"Don't you want a tart?" Juliet asked as he started to walk away.

"Maybe later," he replied as he headed toward the barns.

Life with him wouldn't be difficult, it would be impossible, Amanda told herself. Still, she couldn't get the sound of his laughter or the sight of him smiling out of her mind. Obviously this prairie air had a debilitating effect on the rational portion of her brain. Glancing at her watch, she realized she'd been standing there much too long and quickly returned to her dusting.

Amanda frowned at herself as she collected the dishes from the dinner table. It was dark outside and the family had finished their evening meal, except for Hawk. He hadn't come in yet. Pauline said this was normal, but Amanda found herself worrying about him anyway. He was the last person she should be concerned about, she chided herself.

Carrying a load of dishes, she strode through the door into the kitchen.

"Whoa!" Hawk exclaimed as she collided with him.

Thrown off balance, Amanda teetered. Pieces of silverware clattered to the floor as she fought to keep the dishes balanced. A hand closed around her arm.

"Sorry," Hawk apologized in gruff tones. "I shouldn't have been standing in your path."

She was acutely aware of the strength in his hand as he continued to hold her arm. Even more, his nearness was causing a weakening in her legs. I'm just shaken because I nearly dropped an armload of dishes, she assured herself. Aloud she said, "I should have been watching where I was going."

"I guess we both should be more careful," he replied, his free hand circling the upper portion of her other arm to further steady her.

The contact ignited a heat that swept through her. Looking up, she found herself unexpectedly drawn into the gray-green depths of his eyes. The coldness that was usually there was missing. In its place was concern.

"I guess we should," she managed, having to fight to put together a coherent sentence.

His hold slackened and she expected him to release her. Instead, his touch lingered, becoming something close to a caress, and a tenderness replaced the concern in his gaze. Her breath locked in her lungs. The thought that he might kiss her flashed into her mind. With every fiber of her being, she wanted him to.

Abruptly, like a curtain dropping on a stage, his expression became shuttered and his usual coolness descended over his features. Releasing her, he retreated a step, putting distance between them. Then he turned his back to her and spoke to Pauline.

"I'm going to take a quick shower. Bring my dinner up to my study. I'll eat there. I'm behind in my paperwork." Without looking again at Amanda, he left.

"Are you going to put those plates down or just stand there holding them all night?" Pauline asked.

Amanda's gaze had followed Hawk as he exited the kitchen. Now she jerked her attention back to the cook. "I'm going to put them down," she replied, continuing across the room to the counter.

"You shouldn't let Hawk's gruff manner unnerve you," Pauline instructed sympathetically. "His bark is worse than his bite."

Amanda merely nodded. His gruffness she could handle. It was his tenderness that had shaken her to the core. Glad the cook hadn't been in a position to see what had really happened, Amanda breathed a sigh of relief. But as she returned to pick up the dropped silverware, she admitted she wasn't really sure herself what had happened. For one brief moment, she'd been under the impression Hawk was attracted to her, then he'd shut her out like someone closing a door.

I would be smart to stay away from him, she told herself as she finished clearing the table. But she couldn't get the warmth she'd seen in those gray-green depths out of her mind. They continued to haunt her as she and Pauline began to wash the dishes.

In the middle of scrubbing a pot, Pauline stopped. "Time to fix Hawk's tray," she announced.

"I'll take it up to him." The words were out of Amanda's mouth before she could stop herself. She knew it was silly, but she wanted an excuse to seek out his company.

"I'd appreciate that," Pauline replied, then smiled encouragingly. "And don't let him rattle you this time."

Rattle me! Amanda mused as she carried the tray up the stairs. With just a look, he'd rattled her so badly she couldn't think straight.

Reaching the study, she set the tray on the hall table and knocked. A gruff, "Enter," sounded from the other side.

Obeying, she opened the door, picked up the tray and carried it in. Hawk was seated at his desk. He looked up as she approached. There was only indifference on his face. His thank-you as she set the tray in front of him was purely businesslike.

Leaving the room, she wondered if she'd imagined the tenderness in his gaze. Even if she hadn't, it had been nothing more than a momentary thing and, she told herself, best forgotten. "And forgotten is what it will be," she murmured under her breath.

"I never thought a look could be so hard to forget!" she seethed at her image in the mirror. It was the next morning and she was in the bathroom squeezing toothpaste onto her toothbrush. The faint hint of Hawk's after-shave lingered in the air and was causing a warm, curling sensation in the pit of her stomach while at the same time conjuring up the image of him as he'd steadied her the night before. She began to brush her teeth furiously, counting on the minty taste and smell of the toothpaste to cover the scent of his after-shave.

But as she closed her eyes to wash and rinse her face, the image grew even sharper. Groaning at the idiocy that was causing her to allow this man to occupy so much of her thoughts, she went back to her room and dressed.

As she descended the stairs, she hoped he'd already eaten and left. But luck wasn't with her. He was still sitting at the kitchen table. He looked tired, and concern for him flooded through her. She curtly reminded herself he neither needed nor wanted her concern.

Ignoring him, she greeted Pauline with a chipper "Good morning." Then she crossed to the counter and poured herself a cup of coffee.

"Nice to see someone in a good mood this morning," Pauline said, glancing pointedly at Hawk.

"There's nothing wrong with my mood," he replied. "I just don't feel like talking this morning."

It was obvious to Amanda that the two of them had been arguing about something before her arrival. "I'll just go set the table for breakfast," she said, heading toward the dining room.

"Wait a minute," Pauline ordered. Pausing in the middle of mixing pancake batter, she scowled at Hawk then turned to Amanda. "What do you think of a man who refuses to attend a party his stepmother has been planning for weeks?"

"The party is Jason's idea," Hawk growled. "He wants to show off the ranch to potential buyers."

"But most of the community's going to be here," Pauline rebutted. "And I know of at least two young women who are only coming because they're hoping to see you."

Amanda experienced something that felt very much like jealousy. She shoved the feeling aside. Any woman who wanted Hawk was welcome to him, she told herself.

"I think it would be unwise to encourage Hawk to do anything he doesn't want to do," she said to Pauline. "He'd just stand around glowering and ruin the evening for everyone else."

Pauline breathed a frustrated sigh. "You're probably right."

Amanda couldn't believe she'd been so blunt. Desperate to escape before she said anything else that could embarrass her, she hurried into the dining room. But she did have to admit she'd been wondering if Hawk would be attending Gloria's party. Now she had her answer. Well, his absence should make the evening go a lot more smoothly.

The opening of the dining-room door caught her attention. She turned to see Hawk entering.

"Thanks for coming to my aid," he said, adding dryly, "You weren't what anyone could call flattering, but you did put a stop to Pauline's pestering."

"You're welcome," she replied, returning her attention to the placement of the utensils on the table. She hated the way he made her so uneasy while she, apparently, had no effect on him.

"I brought you something."

She watched him put a wooden whistle hung on a leather thong on the table. It was similar to the one he'd given Juliet. "I suggest that when you go out by yourself, you don't go too far," he continued. "It's easy to get lost. If you do, follow the instructions I gave Juliet. Stay in one place and blow on this."

Swiveling to look at him, Amanda called herself a fool. She'd hoped to see at least a hint of the warmth she'd seen in his eyes the night before, but his demeanor was cool. Frustration filled her. If the man wanted to live out his life alone, that was his business, she told herself, frowning down at the whistle.

"It's more like a flute than a whistle," he continued. "You can make a variety of sounds by covering the holes in different ways. Juliet can show you how it works."

Amanda picked up the whittled instrument intending to give it back to him, but he was already halfway through the door. Well, it could come in handy, she decided and slipped it around her neck, tucking it beneath her shirt.

Chapter Eight

After three days of frantic preparations, the evening of the party had arrived. Amanda moved through the throng of guests in the living room. The stereo had been set up on the patio for those who wanted to dance under the stars. A huge buffet was laid out on the table in the dining room, and the guests were to serve themselves. Other tables with hors d'oeuvres and desserts were placed both in the living room and on the patio. Two bars, each tended by a wrangler dressed in his Sunday best, were set up, one in the living room and one on the patio.

It was Amanda's job to be certain the food was kept in good supply in all locations. She was also to be constantly removing used plates and glasses so that there would be no accumulated messy clutter. Normally she wore jeans or slacks combined with blouses or sweatshirts when performing her duties. However, tonight was a dressy affair, and Mrs. Jerome had provided her with a maid's uniform, consisting of a black, midcalf, long-sleeved, high-necked dress and white, ruffled apron. The dress was a size too big, but Amanda didn't mind. A belt pulled it in at the waist and the blousiness was comfortable.

Smiling politely at guests, Amanda noted that the table by the door leading into the hall needed a new platter of shrimp. But as she changed direction and headed toward it, she stopped abruptly. Hawk had suddenly appeared in the doorway. He was dressed in his blue, pin-striped suit. She recalled the first Sunday he'd come downstairs dressed for church in this clothing. When she'd first noticed the suit in his closet, she'd found herself picturing him in it. In her mind, he'd looked unnatural and uncomfortable. But when she'd actually seen him in it, she'd discovered that her imagined image had been wrong. He wore the suit with the same confident air he wore his work clothes.

He also looked strikingly handsome, she admitted, watching as he joined the party and began to mingle with the guests. A pretty brunette who looked to be in her midtwenties, wearing a sexy red cocktail dress cut low at the top and short at the bottom, made her way to his side and smiled up at him invitingly. Amanda's uniform abruptly went from feeling comfortable to seeming frumpy.

How I look doesn't matter, she chided herself as she forced her attention away from him and back to the nearly empty platter of shrimp. He wasn't going to pay any attention to her. Quickly retrieving the platter, she slipped into the hall and made her way to the kitchen.

When she returned to the living room, she discovered a striking blonde in a clinging blue dress had joined the brunette, and both were attempting to get Hawk to come with them to the patio and dance. He was smiling at them with polite indulgence. Then Amanda saw him leave them and go to talk to an elderly man seated in a corner.

"I don't know if it's because he's such a hunk or such a challenge that I'm so attracted to Hawk," the woman in the red dress confided to the blonde as the two of them approached Amanda and each took a shrimp from the plate she was carrying.

"He's definitely a hunk," the blonde replied, regret strong in her voice as she glanced over her shoulder to where Hawk had gone. "But if you're looking for a commitment, forget it. This ranch is all he cares about."

Picking up another shrimp, the brunette turned back toward Hawk. "I think I'll see if I can change his mind," she said with a seductive gleam in her eyes.

Amanda forced her expression to remain politely bland as she carried the platter to the table. But as she set it down, she couldn't stop herself from glancing out of the corner of her eye in Hawk's direction. The brunette had returned to his side and the blonde had followed. Both women were flirting unabashedly. Hawk, she noted, seemed to be enjoying the attention.

They're welcome to him, she told herself as she picked up some used dishes and glasses then headed again to the kitchen. And if they'd been around him when he was sick, I'll bet they wouldn't be seeking out his company now, she added. Still, she experienced a nagging little pain deep inside when she went out onto the patio a few minutes later and saw him dancing with the brunette. For the rest of the evening, she concentrated on her job and determinedly ignored him.

Amanda yawned, reached for an empty glass, placed it on the tray, then straightened and arched her tired back. It was nearly three in the morning. The party was over. The guests were gone. Everyone else in the household except for her and Pauline had retired. The cook was in the kitchen putting away the leftovers while Amanda gathered up the last dishes and glasses.

"I'll carry that," a male voice said as she finished her stretch and started to lift the heavily laden tray.

Jerking around, she saw Hawk coming through the French doors that led into the living room from the patio. She noticed he'd discarded his suit jacket, removed his tie and unfastened the top two buttons of his shirt. It wasn't fair that he looked so good, she thought grudgingly.

"I thought you'd gone to bed," she snapped, then scowled at herself for sounding curt.

"I didn't think it was fair to leave you and Pauline to do all the cleaning up," he replied, lifting the tray and heading to the kitchen.

"It's our job," she returned, wanting to tell him bluntly to go away and leave her alone, as she grabbed up two more handfuls of plates and followed.

"Well, well, I noticed you broke down and came to the party, after all," Pauline greeted Hawk as he entered the kitchen.

"I decided I'd better look after my interests by keeping an eye on Jason," he replied, setting down the tray.

"I noticed Tina Baker and Jewel Joines keeping an eye on you," Pauline remarked disapprovingly. "Tina treats marriage like a game. I've lost track of how many husbands she's had."

"She's just gotten rid of husband number four," Hawk said with an indifferent shrug, as if the number made no difference to him.

"That's pretty fast work for a woman who's only twenty-eight," Pauline observed. "And Jewel Joines isn't much of a catch, either. Her daddy's spoiled her rotten." The cook's voice became sterner. "And neither of them is cut out to be a rancher's wife. They both prefer city life."

"Then it's a good thing I'm not looking for a wife," he replied with an indulgent grin.

During this exchange, Amanda had been unloading the tray he'd carried in. Now she looked up to see Pauline scowling impatiently at him.

"Well, you should be, and you wouldn't have to look far to find someone real suitable," the cook said pointedly.

Amanda flushed scarlet as Pauline's gaze traveled to her and then back to Hawk. Picking up the empty tray, she quickly headed back out to the patio before the cook could pursue this matchmaking any further. Hawk had said he wasn't looking for a wife, and she knew he meant it. And even if he was, he wasn't looking in her direction.

Behind her, she heard footsteps. Apparently Hawk had chosen a strategic retreat, also. As she set the tray on a table and began gathering dishes and utensils, she hoped he would continue on to his room. Instead, he stopped a short distance behind her.

"I'll carry that in when you have it loaded," he said.

She could feel his gaze almost as if it was a physical touch. Her already tense nerves became even tauter. "That's not necessary. I can handle this on my own."

"I insist," he said without compromise.

She knew arguing would do no good. Besides, she didn't want him to guess how much he affected her. Keeping her back to him, she forced indifference into her voice. "Suit yourself." Then, ordering herself to ignore him, she continued filling the tray.

But ignoring him proved impossible. Even when he stopped watching her and picked up a trash bag into which he began emptying ashtrays and shoving the paper litter left by the guests, she was aware of where he was at any given moment. I just don't want to be bumping into him, she told herself. But when she reached for a glass, the black sleeve of her dress caught her eye and she found herself comparing how she must look to the two sexily clothed women who had pursued Hawk all evening. No wonder he was busy gathering trash, she thought dryly. She was about as femininely appealing as a toad. In the next instant she derided herself for caring about her feminine appeal where Hawk was concerned. The man is making me crazy, she moaned silently in frustration.

Wanting only to get finished so she could be rid of his company, she began to work faster. She was putting a final glass on the tray when unexpectedly the stereo began to play softly. Turning around, she saw Pauline standing beside the machine. The record the cook had chosen was a slow, silky melody.

"Looks like the two of you have gotten this place in good enough shape to leave until morning," Pauline said. Placing herself between Hawk and the tray, she added, "I'm going to take this into the kitchen, and you're going to ask Amanda to dance. She deserves a reward. She worked hard while all the other young people were having fun."

The thought of being held by Hawk caused a current of excitement to race through Amanda. Immediately she scolded herself for this weakness. She was certain he didn't want to dance with her, and she refused to feel any desire to be near a man who didn't want to be near her.

"I'm really too tired," she protested.

"It's late. I suggest we get finished with the straightening and go to bed," Hawk said, confirming Amanda's suspicion that he wasn't the least bit interested in dancing with her. Adding further proof to this, he attempted to pass Pauline and pick up the tray.

"No, you don't." The cook blocked his path solidly. "Tired or not, Amanda deserves to have a moment of fun. You dance with her. I don't like to see those dance lessons I gave you going to waste."

"Those lessons were against my will," he pointed out dryly.

"Someone had to teach you a few social graces," Pauline returned. "'Course, my teachings don't seem to have taken so well. You're embarrassing me, and you're going to make Amanda think she's not attractive."

He was making her feel like a bone that not even the dog wanted, Amanda admitted silently. Aloud, she said with finality, "Mr. Stone's social graces are of no concern to me. I'm going to bed. Good night."

But as she started to move toward the French doors, Hawk's hand closed around her arm. "I'm not going to have any peace for days if you don't dance with me," he said gruffly.

The heat of his touch was traveling up her arm. The desire to know how being held in his embrace felt was strong, but she did have her pride. She met his gaze levelly. "It's not your decision. Pauline can blame me, because I have no interest in dancing with you."

"You're both going to be on my bad side if you don't dance one dance," the cook interjected curtly.

Keeping his hold on Amanda's arm, Hawk tossed Pauline an impatient glance, then returned his attention to Amanda. "We might as well give in. You won't like being on her bad side. She has a way of not talking to you that's worse than being yelled at."

It occurred to Amanda that braving Pauline's wrath might be wiser than allowing herself to be held in Hawk Stone's arms. But curiosity won out. "I suppose," she conceded.

Pauline smiled like a Cheshire cat and walking over to the stereo, started the song at the beginning again.

With an air of resignation, Hawk guided Amanda to the center of the area reserved for dancing. Holding her loosely, he began to lead to the rhythm of the music.

"Never knew two more stubborn young folk," Pauline muttered, loudly enough for them to hear. Then with a final warning glance that dared them to leave the moment she was gone, she moved to the tray, picked it up and strode into the kitchen.

"She'll be watching from the door to make certain we go through with this," Hawk said casting a disgruntled frown in the direction in which the cook had disappeared.

Amanda was irked that he seemed to need an excuse to remain near her. Maybe Pauline's forcing them to dance was a good idea, after all, she decided. By the time the music stopped she was sure to be rid of any lingering attraction she might feel for the rancher. Keeping her posture rigid to avoid as much physical contact as possible, she followed his lead.

Her only contact with Hawk was where her right hand lay loosely in his, and where her left hand rested on his shoulder. Beneath her touch, his muscles felt tense, and as they danced she realized he was holding himself as stiffly as she was holding herself. She grinned dryly. They had to look like a couple of mannequins moving with mechanical rigidity. Suddenly, the urge to laugh bubbled up in her throat. Realizing this was more nerves than humor, she swallowed it.

"You find this amusing?" he demanded.

Evidence of his discomfort was strong in his voice. Again the thought that he considered holding her displeasing caused her temper to flare. Keep cool, she ordered herself. In frosty tones, she said, "I was thinking we should be in a store window in one of those human mannequin displays."

Amanda had been focusing her attention on the third button of his shirt. But as she spoke, she forced herself to glance up at his face. He was looking down at her, and there was a heat in his eyes that made her blood race. Abruptly he shifted his attention to a point somewhere beyond her. But the desire she'd seen remained vivid in her mind.

Thoroughly shaken, her guard collapsed. With her defenses down, she became acutely aware of the feel of his hand flattened against her back. Its imprint burned into her, and she found herself impatient with the fabric of her dress for keeping her from experiencing fully the callused texture of his palm.

Trying to think more clearly, she shifted her attention to her own hand resting on his shoulder. Beneath her palm the muscles were taut. Ordering herself not to behave blatantly, she fought the urge to massage them.

But the control she was exercising over herself was tenuous. The desire to discover how being even nearer to him would feel grew stronger. Prudence warned her to go no further, but she wasn't feeling prudent. She had to know if she was imagining these momentary flashes of attraction she was seeing in his eyes, or if they were real. With the uncertainty of someone fearful of making a fool of herself, she moved closer. She felt a tremor run through him as his hold tightened just enough to accommodate the increased nearness.

Their bodies barely brushed as they danced, but even this fragile contact sent an excitement like none she'd ever experienced before surging through her. The last shred of control she was exercising over her actions snapped and she moved even closer. As the length of her body pressed against his, she could barely breathe. She'd been held by other men, but no previous experience had prepared her for this. Her legs became alarmingly weak and she had an incredibly strong urge to nuzzle his neck.

She laid her head on his shoulder and heard the pounding of his heart. A soft smile spread over her face. She was sure he wasn't as immune to her as he wanted her to believe.

Then abruptly she was being moved away from him and released.

"The song is finished," Hawk announced as he stepped back, putting distance between them.

She looked into his face and saw the heat of passion in his eyes. Triumph filled her. Then abruptly his gaze became shuttered and the cool mask of reserve she was so used to seeing descended over his features.

"Hawk?" She said his name shakily, her voice asking the question she could not put into words.

"I can't offer you what you deserve, Amanda," he said curtly. "I'm an outcast. I have no illusions about ever being fully accepted by either of my people. If I was to marry, my wife would be considered an outcast, too. I would not wish that on anyone."

He was telling her there was no hope for them. Sorrow so intense she wanted to scream jarred her. "Don't you think I should have the right to decide what I want?'' she demanded.

''No,'' came his terse reply. Then he strode past her and into the house.

Amanda stood staring at the French doors through which he'd disappeared. The past few minutes seemed almost surreal. So much had happened and yet the result had left her as she'd been before the dance began. Well, not exactly the same as she'd been, she amended. She'd never felt this intensely frustrated in her life.

Or this embarrassed. She'd practically thrown herself at him. Not practically, she corrected, she *had* thrown herself at him. And he'd tossed her back. He'd also made it perfectly clear he would not change his mind.

''The man makes me crazy!'' she groaned under her breath.

''Well?'' a female voice questioned with interest.

Amanda turned to see Pauline approaching. ''I would appreciate it if you wouldn't try any more of your matchmaking,'' she said firmly.

Pauline grimaced apologetically. ''It went that well, huh?''

''It didn't go at all,'' Amanda replied tersely.

Pauline gave her a motherly smile. ''Some men require a little more prodding than others.''

Amanda moaned inwardly. There was an implication in Pauline's words that the woman was not ready to admit defeat. But Amanda was determined not to be embarrassed again. ''Hawk Stone knows what he wants, and he doesn't want a wife. I want your word that you won't try any more matchmaking, at least not between him and me.''

Pauline snorted. "Hawk's a man worth fighting for.''

"He's also a man who knows what he wants," Amanda rebutted, refusing to allow herself to hope for something that could never be.

"A man's mind can be changed by the right woman," Pauline countered. Then with a nod to give emphasis to this statement, she said, "Good night," and went back inside.

Amanda's jaw trembled as she fought to keep the hot tears filling her eyes from escaping. She'd seen the look of determination on Hawk's face. "Even if Pauline is correct about the right woman being able to change his mind, obviously I'm not that woman," she said, forcing herself to listen to the words in an effort to crush any false illusions that might be lingering in the back of her mind. She'd never behaved foolishly before where a man was concerned and she wasn't going to start now. Telling herself that continuing to think of Hawk would only bring her grief, she went upstairs.

But lying in bed later, she couldn't stop the memory of the dance or what had followed from tormenting her. Again frustration threatened to overwhelm her. In desperation, she assured herself that what she felt for Hawk was superficial—she found him physically attractive and his reticent behavior made him a challenge. But even as she swore this was so, she knew her feelings went deeper. When she'd nursed him through the flu, she'd seen him at his worst. And she'd seen the tender side of him when he was with Juliet. She understood and was willing to accept his gruff side, and just the thought of the tender side filled her with a warmth that enveloped her like a blanket on a cold night. She knew that if he asked her to spend the rest of her life with him, she would agree without hesitation.

"I'm in love with him," she admitted to the darkness surrounding her.

And he *was* a man worth fighting for. Pauline's parting words echoed through her mind. "Maybe I *am* the right woman," she told herself. And maybe, just maybe, Hawk's mind could be changed. It was worth a try.

Chapter Nine

"I can't get used to seeing the boss in a suit." A man's voice speaking in friendly, conversational tones, drifted in through the French doors.

It was the day after the party and Amanda was in the living room doing some final straightening up. A couple of the wranglers were out on the patio stacking chairs and tables to be carried to the storage shed. It was one of them who had spoken. She knew the man was talking about Hawk. Since being at the ranch, she'd learned the ranch hands referred to Jason as Mr. Jerome, to Gloria as Mrs. Jerome and to Hawk as Boss.

"What I can't get used to is takin' orders from a half-breed," a second voice grumbled.

Amanda couldn't stop herself from crossing to the French doors and looking out. The first man who had spoken she recognized as Sam Gordon. He was in his

late forties, and from remarks made by Pauline, she'd
gathered he'd been working on the Jerome ranch for
a long time. He and his wife lived in the foreman's
house, and Mrs. Gordon did the cooking and cleaning for the wranglers. The second man's name was
Richard O'Brian. He was in his early twenties and one
of the newer hands.

Sam straightened and glared threateningly at the
younger man. "Then maybe you'd better be moving
along."

"I didn't mean nothin'," Richard said quickly, his
voice holding an apology.

"You ain't going to find a better boss anywhere,"
Sam continued curtly. "Hawk Stone's a fair and honest man. And he knows ranching as good as his dad."

"Yeah, I know," the younger man replied con-
tritely. "I didn't mean no disrespect. I just meant
takin' orders from him takes a little gettin' used to."

Amanda's hands balled into fists. "Why that
bigot," she seethed. She started to step out onto the
patio to give the younger man a piece of her mind
when a hand caught her arm and jerked her back.
Even before she glanced over her shoulder to see who
had prevented her from venting her anger, she knew
it was Hawk. It shook her to realize just how attuned
she was to his touch. As she turned to face him he released her, and an intense sense of aloneness swept
through her.

"I remember when Jack Jerome trained Hawk to
take over the ranch and then made him foreman,"
Sam was saying sternly, the sound of his voice float-
ing in from the patio to fill the silence between Hawk
and Amanda. "Weren't none of us too happy. Not

only was he half Sioux, he was younger than most of us by a few years. And he was as hard as any man twice his age. From the start he made it clear he wouldn't put up with any slackers. But he always took on the worst tasks himself and never ordered anyone to do a job he wouldn't do himself. He earned the men's respect, and he earned the title of Boss.''

"Yeah, I know,'' Richard conceded. "But he can be a little scary at times, especially when he gets that grim look on his face. You never know what he's thinkin'.''

"I know what I'm thinking,'' Sam snapped impatiently. "I'm thinking that you'd better be grateful you have a job and concentrate on getting these chairs put away.''

The ceasing of conversation followed by the sound of chairs being moved around quickly let Amanda know Richard was taking Sam's advice. As the two wranglers headed off toward the storage shed, she silently studied Hawk's face. His expression was the grim, shuttered one the younger man had just described.

"You'll only bring gossip on yourself if you try to defend me,'' he growled when the two wranglers were out of earshot. "Besides, I don't need or want you to come to my aid.''

If he'd bluntly said, "Stay out of my life,'' his message couldn't have been clearer. Still, she'd promised herself she wouldn't give up too easily. But before she could respond, he turned and strode out of the room in the direction of the hall.

"Trying to befriend that man is like trying to get near a cactus,'' she muttered in frustration.

"Hawk's had a difficult life.''

Amanda swung around to find Gloria Jerome entering the living room from the patio. A look of self-condemnation was on the older woman's face.

"I should have treated him more like a son," she went on. "But I was young and he was an embarrassment to me. I tried not to let my feelings show, but children can sense these things. I was relieved when he left to live with his great-grandfather. When he came back I was jealous because of all the time Jack spent with him. I shouldn't have been. Jack never really opened his heart to Hawk the way he did to Jason and Jasmine."

Defensiveness entered her voice. "But that wasn't all Jack's fault. He wanted Hawk to change his name to Jerome, but Hawk refused. He felt he owed it to his mother to keep her name. Hawk's a very loyal person."

Gloria breathed a sigh. "But maybe Jack would have treated Hawk more tenderly if the boy had been willing to officially become a Jerome. Jack knew Jason wasn't going to want to take over the ranch, and I know he would've liked to have had a son with the Jerome name to carry on."

Surprised that the woman was telling her this, Amanda studied her narrowly. The anxiety in Mrs. Jerome's eyes made her uneasy.

Approaching Amanda, Gloria laid a hand on her shoulder. "Hawk could use a friend right now."

Amanda tensed. She was certain something was going on that was going to hurt Hawk. She also had the distinct impression that Mrs. Jerome was attempting to place the responsibility for Hawk's well-being on her, just as the woman had done when Hawk was ill. But Amanda knew Hawk wasn't any more ready to accept her aid now than he had been then.

Still, she heard herself asking, "What's happened?"

Gloria lifted her hand from Amanda's shoulder and took a step back. Folding her arms in front of her in a defensive manner, she said, "This past winter was especially difficult. We lost a lot of livestock. Hawk keeps a slush fund that will carry the ranch through, and by next year, I've no doubt he'll have it in the black again. But Jason is determined to stick to the letter of the law and exercise our right to sell."

"I thought all four of you had to agree," Amanda said, trying to recall exactly what Pauline had told her.

"If the ranch is losing money, we only need a majority, and Jason and Jasmine want to sell," Gloria replied.

"And you?" Amanda asked, already guessing the answer.

"They're my children. Besides, I've never been as attached to this place as my husband was," Gloria replied. Then with a sigh and a shrug, she turned and left the room.

Amanda stood frozen with indecision. The urge to seek out Hawk and attempt to comfort him was nearly overwhelming. "But if I do, he'll just snap at me," she muttered, thinking that Loco was easier to approach than his insular master.

Nevertheless, she had to do something. Uncertain of how to confront Hawk, Amanda went back to the kitchen to talk to Pauline. Maybe the cook could provide her with a way to breach his defenses, she reasoned hopefully.

"From the look on your face, I'd say that Mrs. Jerome told you, too," Pauline said as Amanda entered.

Amanda nodded.

"That woman." Pauline shook her head with disapproval. "She feels guilty about Hawk, but she's never been able to find a place for him in her heart, so she leaves him for us to comfort."

So Mrs. Jerome had attempted to put the responsibility for Hawk's well-being on Pauline, as well, Amanda thought dryly. Again she was acutely aware of how alone he must have felt in this house. She also realized just how thick the barriers he'd built around himself must have become. A wave of futility washed over her.

"I don't really think he's going to allow anyone to comfort him," she said.

"Probably not," Pauline agreed, then added pointedly, "But *I* am going to try."

Amanda frowned at the accusation in the cook's voice. "I intend to try, too," she said. "But I've already had my head bitten off once by him this morning. I need a little time to regroup before I face another battle."

"He'd probably just come from seeing Mr. Jason," Pauline returned in Hawk's defense.

"Probably," Amanda agreed. Still, she was fairly certain her encounter with Hawk wouldn't have been any different if he'd been having a good day. I'm crazy for trying to win that man, she told herself for the umpteenth time.

Feeling the need to escape, she said, "I've got vacuuming to do," and headed toward the door. But be-

fore she'd taken two steps, Hawk entered. Amanda
came to an abrupt halt. Say something, she ordered
herself, but no words came. She searched his face,
only to discover his shuttered mask was firmly in
place.

Stopping a couple of paces in front of her, he regarded her levelly. "I shouldn't have spoken so harshly
to you this morning. But I didn't see any reason for
you to cause a scene over something so insignifi-
cant."

Hawk had apologized. Amanda could hardly believe it. Maybe there was hope, after all. She wanted
to make him understand she was on his side. "The
man is a bigot," she said. "He should—"

"The world is full of bigots. I prefer to ignore
them," Hawk interrupted in an easy drawl. "I would
also like this subject closed and for you to keep in
mind that I would rather you didn't attempt to cham-
pion me in the future."

Amanda bit back the rest of her words. He was
making it clear once again that he didn't want to have
anything to do with her. And if I was smart, I'd listen, she told herself.

"We're both real sorry to hear about the ranch,"
Pauline said, watching him worriedly.

In spite of the fact that only a moment earlier she
had pointed out to herself that she would be smart to
put this man out of her mind, Amanda immediately
experienced a jab of apprehension.

Hawk shrugged as if to say their sympathy was un-
necessary. "Actually the sale is going to work out well
for me. I've reached an agreement with Jason. Since I
refuse to sell the property my great-grandfather left

me, Jason has agreed that I can keep my fourth of the ranch as long as I take a portion that adjoins the land I already own, cutting a corner out of the ranch and leaving the rest of the land as a single unit. I'll also keep a fourth of the livestock and a portion of the equipment."

"That'll leave you with a comfortable-size spread you can handle on your own," Pauline calculated, clearly looking for a good side to this.

Hawk nodded. "And it'll be a relief not to have Jason always peering over my shoulder." His gaze leveled on Pauline. "I won't be needing a full-time cook, but if you're interested, I could use some weekly help."

"I'll keep that in mind," she replied.

Amanda watched him leave. He'd apologized to her and, realizing that Pauline might be out of work once the ranch was sold, he'd offered her as much of a job as he could afford. Again she had evidence that he wasn't as immune to those around him as he wanted people to believe.

However, he'd also again made it clear he wasn't interested in having her in his life. "Maybe when I thought I saw tenderness and desire in his eyes, I was merely seeing lust," she muttered under her breath as she returned to the living room to vacuum. "And maybe his little speech about being an outcast was just a line to get rid of me, because he realized I'd want more than a one-night fling."

As proof this could be the case, he hadn't shown even the slightest sign of being attracted to her today. In fact, both times she'd seen him this morning, he'd told her to stay out of his life. And that was probably excellent advice, she conceded.

With this thought in mind, she decided the time had come for her to leave. The party was over and Juliet would be going home in a couple of days. But as she switched off the vacuum and started to go in search of Mrs. Jerome to make arrangements for her departure, Hawk's image, uninvited, filled her mind. Her hands balled into fists. In his arms she'd felt an excitement she'd never experienced before. But even more, she'd felt complete, as if that was where she belonged.

"All right, all right. I'll try one last time to win his heart," she said grimly even as she silently called herself a fool.

Amanda drew a deep breath. She was standing outside Hawk's study door with a tray containing a cup of coffee and a piece of pie. It was well past dinnertime.

The meal had been a strain. At Gloria's insistence, Hawk had dined with the family. While she served, Amanda had tried not to eavesdrop on the conversation at the table, but her efforts had been futile. Her concern for Hawk ran too deep for her not to be aware of how he was treated. During the meal, Mrs. Jerome must have thanked him at least half a dozen times for keeping the ranch operating so well during the six years of his tenure. She'd also ordered Jason to allow Hawk to take whatever stock and equipment he wanted.

Amanda frowned as she recalled what had followed that demand.

Jason had scowled at his mother impatiently. "That could cut into our profits tremendously," he'd pointed out sharply.

Mrs. Jerome looked distraught, clearly struggling with her guilt. Obviously a part of her felt she should argue for Hawk's sake, while another part wanted to side with her son.

"I have no intention of taking anything more than my fair share," Hawk had said firmly.

Jason had nodded his approval while Mrs. Jerome had looked relieved.

"After Nana and Uncle Jason move to town, can I still come visit you?" Juliet had suddenly asked, looking hopefully at Hawk.

"That's up to your mother and grandmother," he'd replied, his expression shuttered. Then abruptly, his gaze had softened. "But you'll always be welcome."

"Nana—" Juliet turned to her grandmother. "—can we visit Hawk?"

"Yes, of course," Gloria responded quickly.

A bit too quickly, Amanda noted, certain Mrs. Jerome would make no special effort to see Hawk once the sale had been completed. She glanced toward Hawk, and the dry expression on his face told her he thought the same.

Shortly afterward, he'd excused himself, saying he had a horse he needed to check on.

Later, while she and Pauline had been cleaning up the dishes, he'd come through the kitchen but hadn't paused even long enough to say hello. He'd merely nodded in their direction as he strode past.

"He didn't have any dessert and I made his favorite—strawberry-rhubarb pie," Pauline had said with a worried frown.

"I'll take him up a piece," Amanda had offered.

Now, as she stood outside his study door, she was having second thoughts. Well, if he throws me out one more time, that should get him out of my system once and for all, she reasoned philosophically. She knocked firmly on the door.

A gruff, "Enter," issued from the other side.

Going in, she found him sitting at his desk. "You missed dessert and Pauline spent all afternoon making your favorite."

He'd looked up when she entered, then immediately returned his attention to the ledger in front of him. Without looking at her again, he waved a hand toward a corner of his desk. "Just leave it there."

A part of her wanted to follow his unspoken order and simply set the tray down and leave. But she'd promised herself she'd try one last time to break through the barrier he'd erected around himself.

"Doctors say it isn't healthy to keep emotions bottled up inside," she said. "It can cause ulcers." Mentally she cringed. She'd meant to say something a little more lighthearted—perhaps even something flirtatious. Instead, she'd brought up the subject of his stomach lining.

This time he did look up at her. Impatience flickered in his eyes. "If you're referring to this ranch being sold, I'm not holding back any anger. The truth is, the deal suits me just fine. I'll be my own boss and the ranch I'll be working will be mine."

Amanda had to admit he did appear honestly pleased with the bargain he'd struck with Jason. Not wanting to seem pushy, but determined to have a friendly conversation, she said, "I know you'll be a success."

"I intend to be," he replied with conviction, then in an act of dismissal, he returned his attention to the ledger in front of him.

Amanda ordered herself to leave. It was clear he didn't want to talk to her. But as she started toward the door, a surge of frustration washed through her. Turning back, she scowled at him. "And just what good is all your hard work going to do? So what if you build up the best ranch in South Dakota? You won't have anyone to share your successes with, and no children to leave it to. After you're dead, no one will care." Amanda gasped as she realized what she'd said. An embarrassed flush spread over her face. She couldn't believe she'd been so blunt or so forward. This wasn't like her at all.

His expression was unreadable when he again lifted his head to look at her. "I have a couple of nephews on my mother's side who might be interested in ranching."

Amanda felt like a total fool. Both she and he knew that she'd thrown herself at him again. "I hope they are and you have a good life," she said with stiff formality, and left.

Out in the hall, her cheeks burned from the depth of her embarrassment. She had to get out of this house and away from Hawk before she did something else stupid. It was as if, when she was around him, her conservative nature was suddenly short-circuited.

"I've just never been so attracted to a man before," she seethed under her breath. "Nor felt so frustrated. But this level of emotion can't be real and certainly can't last. It's too intense. Once I'm away from him, I'll laugh at my irrational behavior and forget him," she assured herself.

Going down to the living room, she found Gloria and made arrangements to leave at the end of the week.

Later, up in her room, she glared at her image in the mirror. "You're only going to be here for two more days," she informed her reflection. "Just stay away from Hawk and don't humiliate yourself again."

But as she lay in bed, a nagging apprehension tormented her. It was as if she had unfinished business here that would not allow her to rest. When she'd first arrived, she was sure that finding Juliet had been what had caused her to find her way to the Jerome ranch. Her jaw tensed. She refused to believe that Hawk was the reason she was here. And even if he was, he was *finished* business.

She drew a shaky breath. There was one other thing—Hawk's gold mine. Maybe that was what she was supposed to find. Thinking about it, this seemed the most logical explanation. Her talent had always been to find *things,* rather than people.

Resolve etched itself into her features. She wasn't going to have any peace until she discovered what had brought her here. Tomorrow was her afternoon off. She'd go for a ride and see if she could find the mine.

"But even if I don't," she vowed, "I'm leaving here Saturday morning and never looking back."

Chapter Ten

"This is probably the dumbest thing I've done yet," Amanda groaned.

As soon as she'd finished with the lunch dishes, she'd gone to her room, gotten the necklace Hawk had given her and put it on. Then she'd had one of the wranglers saddle her a horse, and she'd ridden off in the direction of Hawk's property. She wasn't even sure how she would know when she reached his land. According to Pauline, to increase the acreage Jerome cattle could graze on, the fences between the two properties had been torn down soon after Speckled Owl had died.

"If I was going to find the mine, surely I would have found it before today," she chided herself. Still, she reasoned, it was a nice afternoon for a ride, and since this would be her last, she might as well enjoy it.

Noting landmarks as she rode, to help her find her way back, she let the horse set an easy gait. She'd miss this untamed land, she thought with regret. But she wouldn't miss Hawk Stone, she added quickly. The necklace suddenly felt unexpectedly heavy, and she reached up to touch it. But no images stirred in her mind.

"This is ridiculous!" she grumbled, furious at herself for even considering the possibility that the necklace would lead her to the mine. If it had been going to, it would have done so the first time she'd held it. Instead, she'd seen Hawk as a young boy grieving over his great-grandfather. Now she saw nothing. But the memory of the grief-stricken boy tore at her. Suddenly, in her mind's eye, she saw Hawk looking at her with a longing that took her breath away. That, she admonished herself, was purely wishful thinking.

"Forget him," she ordered out loud, using the sound of her voice to give emphasis to this command. "Just concentrate on the scenery."

As she forced him out of her mind, her horse snorted and came to an abrupt halt. Amanda glanced around, wondering what had caused this behavior. She saw nothing to explain the horse's actions.

"Everything's all right, girl," she assured the mare, gently stroking her neck in a soothing manner. Beneath her hand, she felt the animal's muscles tense even more. Then she heard a catlike snarl and caught a glimpse of movement to her left. The mare reared up in fear. In the next instant Amanda was holding on for her life as the spooked animal took off at a gallop.

"Whoa!" she yelled, clinging to the reins and saddle horn. But the animal refused to heed her command.

The prairie passed in a blur as she fought back panic and tried to maintain her seat in the saddle. Ahead she saw a narrow, shallow ravine. She wasn't sure if she should hold on more tightly or get ready to jump clear. If the horse's timing was off, it would step in the ravine, trip and fall. But before Amanda could decide on what action to take, the horse leapt and landed safely on the other side.

Amanda bounced hard in the saddle and her left foot came out of the stirrup. She tried to get it back in, but her balance had been lost. When the mare made a jerking turn around the base of a particularly high hill, she slid precariously to one side. She lost her grip and with a frightened scream fell to the ground.

"Ouch," she moaned, grimacing with pain. Her rear end and left leg had taken the brunt of the fall. But every inch of her had felt the jolt. Now she lay flat on her back trying to get her breath. When her gasping subsided and she was breathing normally, she wiggled her toes to see if they still worked. They did. Slowly she shifted into a sitting position. To her relief, nothing seemed to be broken. Her gaze traveled over the surrounding landscape. Rolling, deserted prairie stretched out around her on three sides. To her right was the sharply rising hill that had caused her final loss of balance.

She eased herself to her feet and dusted off her jeans and shirt. A tenderness on her hip told her she was going to have a bruise to remember this ride by. "An idiot on a fool's errand should expect to end up in a mess like this," she chided herself.

She bit her lip in indecision. She could walk back to the ranch. But as she took a step, sharp little pains jabbed at her. She also had to admit she wasn't totally sure which direction to head in. She hadn't had much time to note any landmarks during her wild ride. The wrangler who had saddled her horse had told her that if she did get lost to just give the horse its head and it would find its way home. Therefore, she decided, it was logical to assume the horse, now no longer in sight, would eventually go back to the ranch. Then they'd send out a search party for her. And hadn't Hawk told her that if she did get lost, the best thing to do would be to stay put?

Having had this little discussion with herself, she looked around for a comfortable place to wait. A medium-size boulder resting against the side of the hill, looked inviting. Crossing to it, she sat down and leaned her back against it to wait. An hour dragged by. The thought that maybe she should try to walk back to the ranch again played through her mind. But when she started to get to her feet, her muscles rebelled. Groaning at the knowledge that she would probably be stiff for days, she shifted to a more comfortable position and resumed her wait.

Bored, she remembered the flutelike whistle Hawk had given her. Operating on the theory that if she had it with her, she probably wouldn't need it, she'd worn it along with the necklace. "So much for the theory that an umbrella wards off the rain," she muttered, toying with the primitive instrument.

Trying not to consider the possibility of not being found before dark, she began to blow little tunes on it. She was thinking she was actually beginning to sound fairly good when she heard a horse whinny. Shading her eyes with her hands, she gazed in the direction of the sound and saw a rider coming. Even as far away as they were, she recognized Hawk and Loco.

She rolled her eyes skyward. "Why couldn't I have been found by someone else?" she grumbled. "Anyone else?"

Reining in a few feet from the boulder, Hawk said nothing as he pulled out his rifle, fired a couple of shots, then resheathed it. Amanda saw the anger etched deep into his face. As he dismounted he remained silent, and it occurred to her that he considered having to come looking for her such a tremendous nuisance he was too furious to speak. Well, she hadn't asked him to come rescue her, she fumed silently.

Hawk stood regarding her narrowly. At last he demanded harshly, "What in the hell are you doing all the way out here on my land?"

"I didn't choose to be here," she replied, her shoulders squared with dignity. "My horse got spooked and chose her own destination. I just didn't manage to stay on for the full ride."

His gaze raked her. "Are you injured?"

She searched his face for some sign of concern. All she saw was controlled anger. Well, this should certainly cure me of caring for him, she told herself. He clearly didn't care about her.

"Just a few bruises," she said. Keeping her jaw taut so as not to allow even a modicum of pain to show, she got to her feet.

"I thought I suggested you not go riding alone," he growled.

She'd never liked being patronized and she especially didn't like it when Hawk was the one doing it. She met his glare with haughty self-righteousness. "No one was around. Besides, I wanted to go out alone."

His tone was condemning. "Do you have any idea how much trouble you've caused? I've got work to do. I don't have time to spend my days scouring the prairie for lost females."

In spite of her efforts not to view anything he said as important, this proof that he saw her as a monumental nuisance cut too deeply. Her effort to treat him with cool indifference collapsed.

"Then you should have let someone else come find me," she shot back.

The ire in his eyes grew stronger. "None of the others know how to track well enough. You'd have been out here all night."

That he'd only come to her rescue because no one else could have found her so quickly added salt to the wound. "I suppose you think I owe you my undying gratitude," she returned curtly. "And an apology for pulling you away from more important things."

His jaw tensed as if he was having a struggle controlling his rage. "All I want from you is your word that you won't go off by yourself again."

Her shoulders straightened even more. "You don't have to concern yourself. I'm leaving Saturday. This was my last ride."

"Good."

She saw a flash of relief on his face. He was glad she was going! Hurt spread through her, and she realized that a small, foolish part of her had been clinging to a shred of hope that she would see some regret. *Idiot! Idiot! Idiot!* she screamed in silent fury at herself.

He drew an impatient breath. "Come on," he ordered, waving her to him.

She realized he intended for her to ride double back to the ranch. Rebelling at the thought of being any nearer to him than she was at that moment, she tossed him a "get lost" glance and sat back down next to the boulder.

"I'll just wait for the next bus," she said. "In rancher's terms that means you can send someone else with a horse for me."

The scowl on his face deepened. "That would be a waste of time and energy. Now get to your feet and get up onto Loco."

"I've got nothing against your horse, but his rider can go to hell," she snapped back, remaining firmly seated.

For a long moment, he stood indecisively. Then in a couple of strides he bridged the distance between them. His expression one of intense irritation, he reached down and circled her waist with his hands and lifted her to her feet.

"Either you walk to that horse or I'll carry you," he threatened.

He'd released her the moment she was standing, making her feel as if he'd detested the contact. Pride glistened in her eyes. "I am not getting onto your horse and don't you dare touch me again," she warned rawly.

"I'm not leaving you out here," he growled back.

"You," she snapped, "have no choice. I am the master of my fate and I'll make my own decision about who I want to be rescued by."

Deep inside, she knew she sounded childish, but she couldn't help herself. It hurt to have him treat her like a nuisance and an irritant. Her jaw set in a firm line, she began to sit again.

Hawk's hand closed around her arm. "Damn you, Amanda," he snarled.

She wanted to tell him to let go of her, but before she could speak, his free hand cupped the back of her head and his mouth found hers.

The contact was powerful, hungry and demanding. For a moment she was too stunned to react, then a blazing fire swept through her, and winding her arms around him, she added her own strength to the kiss. Her body molded against his, and every fiber of her being reveled with delight and excitement.

His hold on her tightened until she could barely get her breath, but she didn't care. Here in Hawk's arms was where she belonged. She knew that with the same certainty she knew the sun would rise and set.

Suddenly she was thrust away. Her arms were captured and gently but firmly forced from around his neck to her sides. Opening her eyes, she saw Hawk's expression go from self-condemnation to disgust.

"Now that I have your attention," he said gruffly, "you're going to do as I say!" He swung up into the saddle, then reached down to give her a hand up. "Get up on this horse," he ordered.

Too shaken to fight him, she mounted behind him. But as her arms circled him, she felt his muscles tense.

The self-condemnation and disgust she'd seen on his face a few moments earlier registered more fully. He regretted having kissed her. That was obvious. Even more, he'd implied that he'd only done it to make her obey. Her nerves snapped.

"You don't have to act as if you just kissed a toad," she seethed.

"It'd be best if we both forgot what happened just now," he returned, his voice carrying a command.

She scowled at his back. "That suits me just fine."

"Good," was his curt response. He gave Loco a nudge and they started back to the ranch.

Riding behind him, Amanda was furious at herself. She couldn't believe that in spite of her determination to feel only indifference or anger toward him, each time she brushed up against him, embers of a fire deep within her were fanned until a slow burn began to spread through her. Attempting to fight this disturbing effect, she held on to him as lightly as possible.

They had gone only a short distance when he abruptly reined Loco to a halt. "Stop that," he growled.

Startled, she frowned at the back of his head. "Stop what?"

"Just get a tight grip on my shirt or belt," he ordered.

As she gripped the cotton fabric of his shirt, she studied his rigid back. She'd been concentrating so hard on controlling her reactions to him she hadn't noticed his to her. She'd assumed he was having none. She'd assumed he was stoically ignoring her presence. Now she realized she'd been wrong. In her attempt to hold him lightly, her hands had moved gently against him. The touch had clearly made him uneasy.

She recalled the kiss. There had been a hunger there, and the way he'd crushed her to him had certainly felt like more than a ploy to get her attention. The look of passion she'd seen in his eyes the night they'd danced again played through her mind. Her mouth formed a thoughtful pout as the suspicion that he was as attracted to her as she was to him grew stronger. It was possible, she reasoned, that his determination to stand alone was making him refuse to admit how he really felt.

On the other hand, this could be all wishful thinking and she could be setting herself up to look foolish again, she warned herself. But again she chose to ignore the warning. She had to know the truth once and for all. Releasing her hold on his shirt, she flattened her hands against his chest. Beneath her palms, she felt his muscles tauten. She leaned up against his back, and he straightened until he was ramrod stiff. It was like holding on to a marble statue. But instead of the coldness of stone, a heat radiated from his body. The embers deep within her were rekindled, and with her body pressed softly to his, she felt his breathing grow ragged.

"You're not as immune to me as you want me to believe," she said, her voice daring him to deny this.

Hawk drew a harsh breath. "No, I'm not."

A surge of triumph swept through her and she wanted to shout with joy. Instead, she kissed his shoulder. Then, freeing one hand, she moved his thick black hair aside and kissed his neck.

"Stop that!" he ordered.

"Caring for someone isn't so horrible," she assured him. Playfully running the tip of her tongue a short distance along one of the taut cords of his neck, she added, "You taste sort of salty." Feeling him tremble, she smiled and kissed him again.

He reined Loco to a halt. Sure she had broken down his barriers, she waited expectantly for him to turn and kiss her. But when he shifted in the saddle so he could look back at her, his expression was cold.

"I have no intention of taking you as a wife," he said bluntly.

Hurt and humiliation flooded through her. Hot tears burned at the back of her eyes. She'd made a fool of herself again! Pride commanded her to say something flippant that would imply she wasn't interested in marrying him, but no words could get around the gigantic lump in her throat.

"It's nothing personal," he continued gruffly. "You're cute and you can be pleasant to have around when you're not being stubborn. I'm just not in the market for a wife, and I wouldn't ask you to settle for anything less."

Bile rose in her throat. He was patronizing her again. "I suppose I should thank you for rescuing me a second time this afternoon," she said dryly. "You'd make a terrible husband. This prairie air has clearly affected my rational thinking." She suddenly wanted to be away from him. "I'll walk the rest of the way back. Obviously that fall I took jarred me more than I thought. I need a little time to clear my head and let sanity return."

He caught her before she could dismount. "Whatever spooked your horse is still out here. Now just behave and let me get you back to the ranch."

Rebellion bubbled up inside her, but she held it in check. She already looked foolish. Insisting on walking would make her look even more so. "Fine," she agreed between clenched teeth.

Hawk turned to face the front again and nudged Loco into motion. Wanting as little contact with him as possible, Amanda hooked her fingers through a couple of the loops on his jeans so that the barrier of a leather belt was between them. If after they got back to the ranch she never saw Hawk Stone again, she'd die happy, she assured herself.

Hawk said nothing as they rode. When they reached the ranch, he took her all the way to the steps leading to the kitchen door. The moment he reined Loco in, she slipped off the horse's back. But as she lifted her leg to put her foot up on the first step, a pain shot up her thigh and she was forced to grab the railing to keep from falling.

In the next instant Hawk had dismounted and was scooping her up in his arms. "You did get injured," he snarled accusingly as he started up the stairs with her.

"I got bruised and shaken and I got stiff while I was on Loco, that's all," she hissed back. "Now put me down!"

Ignoring her, he kicked at the screen door. "Pauline, open up," he yelled.

"I see you found her," the cook said, hurrying to obey. Anxiety spread over her face. "Is she badly injured?"

"I'm not injured at all!" Amanda replied. Glaring at Hawk, she said again, "Put me down!"

Ignoring her, Hawk continued through the kitchen. "Call the doctor. I want her checked thoroughly," he ordered Pauline as he went.

Amanda countermanded his order over his shoulder. "Don't call a doctor. I don't need one." She glared up at Hawk. "Put me down!"

"Amanda!" Gloria Jerome looked panicked as Hawk nearly collided with her on his way out of the kitchen. The woman stepped to one side to allow him to pass. Falling into step behind him, she asked, "Is she hurt badly?"

"I'm not hurt at all," Amanda insisted over Hawk's shoulder. "Just a little bruised," she amended.

"Then why is Hawk carrying you?" a young voice asked.

Amanda looked down to see Juliet jogging along beside her grandmother. Her gaze shifted back to Hawk. For a man who claimed to have no real feelings for her, he did seem to be showing an exaggerated concern.

Hawk's jaw hardened. "She's been injured, and since I'm responsible for the employees of this ranch, it's my duty to see she gets the proper care."

Amanda wanted to tell him what he could do with his sense of duty, but there was a child present. Clamping her mouth shut, she said nothing as he carried her into her room and laid her on the bed.

Looking down at her, his expression was the same cool, detached one she remembered from their very first encounter. "Goodbye, Amanda," he said with finality, then left.

"Where do you hurt?" Gloria demanded, reaching the bed as Hawk walked away.

Amanda looked up into the concerned faces of the older woman and child. "Really, I'm only a little shaken. I'm sure that after a hot bath, I'll be fine."

"You will stay there until the doctor comes to look you over," Hawk ordered from the doorway. His gaze leveled on Gloria. "I'm leaving her in your care."

Amanda lay still, listening to his bootsteps going along the hall and then down the stairs. Once she was sure he was out of earshot, she shifted into a sitting position.

"Now, if you ladies will excuse me," she said, "I'm going to soak in a hot bath. And—" she looked Mrs. Jerome in the eye "—cancel the doctor."

"I will not," Gloria replied. "Hawk's right. You're our responsibility."

Amanda motioned the woman and child back, then rose to her feet. "Having the doctor come out here is a waste of time."

"You're as stubborn as Hawk," Gloria accused, watching her anxiously.

Amanda turned to face her. "No one is as stubborn as Hawk." Then brushing past Gloria, Amanda grabbed her robe from the closet and headed to the bathroom.

She was lying soaking in the hot water a while later when a knock sounded on the door. "The doctor's here," Pauline informed her through the barrier.

"I don't need a doctor," Amanda called back. "I've just got a couple of bruises. They aren't even as bad as I thought they might be."

"Well, he's here, so you might as well let him check you over," Pauline persisted.

Amanda admitted to herself that normally she would have given in just to be polite. After all, the doctor had driven all the way out here to the ranch. But the fact that Hawk had ordered her to be seen grated on her. Rebellion swelled in her.

"Tell the doctor to send me a bill for his trouble, but that I'm too comfortable in here to take time out to be examined for imaginary injuries."

"Amanda, get out of that tub this minute!" Hawk roared through the door.

In spite of the relaxing effect of the hot water, her body tensed. She'd been sure he'd left the house. "Go away!" she hollered back.

"Either you get out or I'm coming in and getting you out," he threatened.

Amanda scowled at the door. She had no doubt he meant what he said. She'd already placed herself in humiliating positions in front of him one too many times. She wasn't about to do it again.

"All right," she said grudgingly. "I'm getting out."

About forty minutes later, she made her way with only a slight limp down the stairs. The doctor had confirmed her own diagnosis that, other than a few bruises, she was fine. Now he was gone and she was going back to work. Entering the kitchen, she glanced around guardedly.

"If you're looking for Hawk, he isn't here," Pauline said. "As soon as the doctor came down and reported that you were fine, he left for his place. Said he wouldn't be back until Sunday."

Amanda breathed a sigh of relief. At least she wouldn't have to face him again.

Putting aside the knife she was using to slice her homemade bread, Pauline studied Amanda. "Do you want to talk about whatever happened between the two of you?" she coaxed.

"Nothing happened," Amanda replied. The sudden memory of Hawk's kiss washed over her and her stomach knotted. He was determined not to feel anything beyond lust, she reminded herself, and when Hawk made up his mind, his resolve was unshakable. "At least, nothing of consequence," she added firmly.

"I don't mean to be offensive, but you look like you've been through a war," Pauline persisted. "And since the two of you got back, Hawk's actions haven't been making much sense, either. He was so concerned about your welfare he paced the kitchen floor the entire time Dr. Franklin was with you. And even after the doctor came down and said you were fine, Hawk grilled him to make certain the doctor had honestly checked you over and not let you dissuade him from doing the examination. Then after the doctor left, Hawk suddenly decided he needed to get away for a few days." Pauline shook her head. "Something must have happened. That man was running away, and I've never seen him run away from anything before."

Amanda wanted to feel some hope that Hawk might honestly care for her and that it was his fear of not being able to control those feelings that had caused him to leave. But she refused to play the fool again. She guessed he had most likely gone up to his place to save them both from her embarrassing antics.

"Hawk knows what he wants," she said, then went into the dining room to set the table.

But as she served dinner, she grew more and more tense. She felt out of place. Following the meal, while she helped Pauline with the dishes, the need to leave the ranch grew too strong to resist. When she was finally finished for the day, she went in search of Gloria Jerome.

"I'd like to leave tomorrow morning," she said.

Gloria gave her no argument. She thanked Amanda, paid her and wished her well.

"And that's that," Amanda said under her breath as she went to her room. Wanting an early start, she began to pack.

A knock on her door interrupted her task. When she answered it, she discovered Juliet there.

"Nana said you were leaving. I've come to say goodbye," the little girl said.

Amanda squatted down to Juliet's eye level and held out her hand. "It's been a pleasure knowing you," she said with a smile as she shook the child's hand.

"It's been a pleasure knowing you, too," Juliet replied with a grin. Then the grin turned to a frown. "I'm going to miss you. Hawk's going to miss you, too."

Amanda grimaced. "I doubt very much that he will miss me."

"He watched you all the time," Juliet said with authority. "I saw him. He didn't think anyone saw him, but I did."

Again Amanda fought back the hope that Hawk might care for her. Even if he did, he wasn't going to admit it. "He was probably just worried I might steal the silver," she said.

Juliet looked horrified. "You wouldn't do anything like that!"

"No. I was just making a joke," Amanda assured her.

Relief spread over Juliet's features. "I've got to go to bed now," she said. "Good night."

"Good night," Amanda replied, and waved as the child trotted off down the hall.

Straightening, Amanda closed the door, then returned to her packing. But as she snapped the final suitcase shut, the feeling that she was leaving something undone continued to haunt her. She'd left the necklace and the whistle out on the dresser to have Pauline return them to Hawk. Now she was irresistibly drawn to them. Tentatively her fingers touched the beads of the necklace. Twice she'd tried to use it to find Hawk's gold mine and twice she'd failed.

"The gold mine has to be my unfinished business here," she reasoned aloud. "And the third time is supposed to be the charmed one."

She switched off the lights so that only moonlight illuminated the room. Then picking up the necklace, she carried it to the chair by the window. She sat and, holding the necklace in her hands, concentrated.

The boulder she'd leaned against that afternoon filled her mind. Her back stiffened. She would not remember Hawk's kiss, not now, not ever. "Think *gold mine*," she ordered herself through clenched teeth.

The image of the boulder remained. A man's figure began to form beside it. Certain Hawk was whom she would see, a wave of frustration washed over her. But it wasn't Hawk. The man she saw was the Sioux she'd first seen wearing the necklace. While she watched, he went to the boulder and, using a long pole as a lever, began to move the rock. An opening barely large enough for a man to squirm through was exposed. Laying aside the long pole, he turned and smiled at her. She read gratitude on his face and had the feeling that a burden had been lifted from his shoulders. Then he faded from her view.

Opening her eyes, she leaned back and took a deep breath. She noticed her hands were damp from perspiration and her forehead was beaded with cold sweat. Her body felt drained and she was ravenously hungry.

"I did it!" she breathed. Exhilaration filled her. For the first time, she'd actually been able to control her talent.

"And now I need some food," she said, rising from the chair. After she'd eaten, she'd write Hawk a note telling him where to find his lost mine. Tomorrow morning she'd give the note, the whistle and the necklace to Pauline to give to him. That would put an end to this episode of her life. And an end to the quest the diary had sent her on. Her aimless seeking had brought her nothing but frustration. It was time to return to a more rational existence. It was time to go home.

"And never look back," she ordered herself as she headed to the kitchen.

Chapter Eleven

Amanda drew a shaky breath. Last night, even as she'd sat writing Hawk the note giving directions to the location of his mine, she'd known she wasn't going to leave the message with Pauline to give to him. She had tried. This morning after she'd packed her car, she'd carried the necklace, whistle and note with her when she'd gone into the kitchen to say goodbye to the cook, but they'd remained in her possession.

"This is something I have to finish myself," she murmured as she drove toward Hawk's place. But seeing the small ranch house in the distance, she tensed. Dawn had barely broken over the horizon when she'd left the Jerome homestead. Morning shadows stretched across the prairie. The thought that maybe he would still be asleep crossed her mind. If so, she would leave the note, necklace and whistle where he would find them and be on her way.

Loco reared and whinnied as she parked and got out of her car.

"Good morning to you, too," she greeted the stallion. Approaching the corral, she was surprised when Loco trotted over to her. She reached out and stroked his neck. "You take care of yourself," she said. Then heard herself adding, "And take care of Hawk."

The moment these words were out, she scowled at herself. Hawk didn't need or want beast or human to take care of him.

"You're up early," a male voice said from behind her.

She turned to see Hawk coming toward her and knew this was the real reason she'd come—she'd wanted to see him one last time. She couldn't believe the extent of the weakness she had for this man. Self-directed anger filled her.

"I decided to leave today and wanted to get an early start," she replied.

A hint of impatient reprimand suddenly flashed in his eyes. "I hope this time you'll be more careful about not getting lost. You'd be wise to follow your map more closely in the future and stick to the main roads while you seek your destiny."

She glared at him. He didn't want her in his life, but he felt free to tell her how to live hers. Don't lose your temper, she ordered herself. Do this with dignity.

"I've decided this expedition is nothing more than a silly whim," she said coolly. "I'm going home and sending the diary back to my cousin. Then I'll find myself a nice, conservative husband, have two children and live happily ever after."

The cool mask of indifference she was so used to seeing descended on Hawk's face. "That sounds like an excellent plan."

A tremor of pain shot through her. In spite of all the evidence she had to the contrary, she was forced to confess she'd allowed Pauline's talk about his running away and Juliet's claim that Hawk had shown an unusual amount of interest in her to give her encouragement. She'd come up here hoping that when he realized she was really going to leave, he would not be able to bear seeing her go. Romantic fool! she mocked herself. The need to get away from him was suddenly overwhelming.

Remembering she'd left the necklace along with the note and whistle on the passenger seat of her car, she headed to the vehicle. "I came by to tell you something," she said over her shoulder as she reached the car and jerked the driver's door open. Wanting to make a quick getaway when she was through, she slipped in behind the wheel and closed the door.

He'd followed her and come to a halt within about four feet of the car.

His determination to keep a distance between them was not lost on her. In all fairness, she couldn't fault him. He'd never lied to her or led her on.

Just tell him what you came to tell him and get out of here, she ordered herself. Aloud she said, "I think your lost mine is behind the boulder you found me leaning against yesterday. You'll need a sturdy pole to lever it out of place."

She'd expected him to exhibit at least a small amount of excitement, but his expression remained stoic. "I'll check into it," he said.

She recalled that he'd told her several times he thought that even if the mine actually existed, he believed it was played out. Even more likely, he probably didn't believe she was right about the location, she decided. Well, she'd done her part. There was only one thing left. She closed her hand around the necklace, then extended the beaded ornament out the window.

"This belongs to you," she said flatly.

Still maintaining his distance, he frowned impatiently as if to say they'd had this conversation before. "I gave it to you. It's yours."

"I'd prefer not to have anything to remind me of you," she returned, then heard herself adding, "Someday you'll regret not keeping me in your life."

Immediately she blushed scarlet. She couldn't believe she'd said that. She tossed the necklace in his direction, started the engine and drove away.

"Well, that sure wasn't the calm, dignified ending I'd planned," she chided herself as she reached the main road. But it was an ending. She drew a shaky breath. She couldn't believe she'd once more thrown herself at him so blatantly. Well, at least she'd never have to face him again.

An object on the seat beside her caught her eye. The whistle had edged its way out from under the note. She groaned at the sight of it. Well, she wasn't going back just to return it. Her jaw firmed with decision. She'd throw it away at her first stop. And, she added curtly, that would put an end to the lingering feeling that she still had unfinished business here.

* * *

Hawk rode out to the boulder. When Amanda had told him the location of the mine, he'd believed she'd truly found it. What he didn't know was if there was any gold left. Using the pole he'd brought with him, he moved the large rock. Behind it, he saw the opening. Lying on his stomach, he held his flashlight ahead of him as he worked his way inside. The passage had a gentle downward slope. For about ten feet he had to stay on his stomach and work his away along in a snakelike movement. Then abruptly the narrow passage opened into a long cavern just high enough for him to stand upright. A couple of pick axes, their handles rotted from age and their metal parts rusted, lay near his feet. Several deep alcoves marked the spots where the walls had been mined. Taking his knife, he scraped it over the rocky surface and saw the glisten of gold.

Amanda sat cross-legged on the window seat in her bedroom at her parents' home. It was now three weeks since she'd arrived back in Seattle.

She had two job interviews lined up during the next couple of days for positions with major accounting firms. Both were callbacks and looked promising. In the meantime she'd been working as a waitress at a restaurant where the tips were good. A girlfriend she got along with very well was losing her apartment mate and had offered to share her place with Amanda. All in all, Amanda had to admit, her life was back on track.

The problem was it didn't feel back on track. She was edgy and at loose ends. In her hands she was

holding the whistle Hawk had made. When she'd
stopped that first night on her way home, she'd intended to throw it away. But when the time had come,
she couldn't. She'd told herself that tossing it would
be wasteful, and so decided to keep it and give it to her
nephew. When she'd reached home, she'd reasoned
that her nephew was too young. After all, he was only
two. So she'd kept it to give to him when he got older.
Now she was sitting toying with it. Putting it to her
lips, she played a tune she'd made up that day by the
rock. Her chin trembled and she found herself wish-
ing she could look up and see Hawk. In the next instant she was scowling at herself.

Drawing a tired breath, she faced the truth. Neither Juliet nor the gold mine had been the real reason
her talent had taken her to the Jerome ranch. Hawk
had been what she'd been seeking. But he hadn't
wanted to be found.

She blew a shrill note on the whistle. "I've got to
put that man out of my mind!" she growled at herself.

The sound of footsteps rushing hurriedly down the
hall caught her attention. The door was suddenly
thrust open. "Are you all right?" her mother demanded. "What was that sound?"

"Just a whistle. Sorry I..." Amanda's apology died
on her lips. Beyond her mother she saw Hawk Stone.
He was dressed in his blue suit. He even had on his tie.
Sure this was an hallucination, she blinked. But when
she opened her eyes, he was still there. She suddenly
felt acutely grubby. She'd spent the morning cleaning
and was still dressed in her old shorts and shirt. If she
ever saw Hawk again, she'd wanted to look impres-

sive. But then nothing that had to do with her and Hawk Stone had worked out the way she'd hoped it would.

Following the line of her daughter's vision, Leigh MacGreggor looked over her shoulder. "Mr. Stone, I thought I asked you to wait in the living room," she said sternly, clearly startled to find him behind her.

"I heard the whistle. I thought Amanda might need help," he replied stiffly.

Say something! Do something before you begin to look like a tongue-tied teenager! Amanda ordered herself silently. "I meant to return this to you," she said, rising from the window seat and moving toward the door. But she didn't trust herself to get too close to him. In spite of her efforts to feel nothing, just the sight of him was causing an aching within her. But she refused to allow herself to even hope he'd come to ask her to share his life. The pain of previous disappointments was too strong. Stopping while still inside her room, she handed the whistle to her mother who was standing in the doorway.

"Would you give this to Mr. Stone for me?" she requested.

As if not quite certain what was going on, Leigh MacGreggor accepted the whistle and turned to give it to Hawk.

"That belongs to Amanda," he said, refusing to accept it. Then, reaching into his pocket, he pulled out the beaded necklace and handed it to Leigh Mac-Greggor. "So does this. Will you give it to her, please? She deserves it." His gaze swung to Amanda. "I found the gold mine. There was enough there for me to purchase the ranch."

Leigh's eyes rounded with interest. "Gold mine?"

"I'll tell you about it later," Amanda assured her mother, her gaze not leaving Hawk's. She was furious that he'd come here merely to thank her. Didn't he know how much just the sight of him hurt her? "I'm glad for you, Hawk. But I don't want your thanks or your gifts," she said with dismissal.

Leigh was still standing between the two of them. She looked from Hawk to her daughter, then down at the whistle and necklace she was holding. "Obviously this is something the two of you need to work out on your own," she said, handing the whistle back to Amanda and the necklace back to Hawk. "I'm sure I've got something I need to do downstairs. I'll figure out what when I get there." With a final glance at her daughter and then the rancher, she left.

As her mother headed down the hall, Amanda stood facing Hawk. She wanted to feel nothing but indifference. Instead, the urge to move closer to him and gently stroke his jaw was close to overwhelming. Don't behave like a fool again, she admonished herself. Fighting to maintain a cool facade, she balled her hands into fists and squared her shoulders.

"There was no reason for you to come all this way to thank me. But since you did, you can now consider your duty done and leave." She reached for the door, intending to close it and shut him from her view.

Hawk stepped forward and placed his hand against the wooden barrier. "I didn't come here just to thank you."

"Why then?" she demanded, his nearness causing her control to crumble. "Did you miss seeing me look like an idiot by throwing myself at you every time I opened my mouth?'' A flush of embarrassment reddened her cheeks, but she ignored it. Pride glistened in her eyes as she faced him angrily.

"I've missed you," he said gruffly.

Amanda's breath caught in her lungs. Terror that this was merely a dream filled her. Or maybe he hadn't meant what he'd said in the way she wanted him to mean it. She studied his face. His expression was guarded. Wait to hear what else he has to say before you start hoping for too much, she cautioned herself.

He shifted uneasily, then his jaw firmed with purpose. "Pauline says I made a decision for you that I should have let you make."

"What decision was that?" she asked, feeling as if her whole world rested on his answer.

He regarded her narrowly. "I warned you once that any woman who chose to stand by me could find herself being subjected to prejudice."

"I have never allowed my life to be ruled by small-minded people," she replied, her blood beginning to race.

"And I know I'm not an easy man to get along with," he continued, clearly intent on pointing out all the negatives.

"You do have a stubborn streak that can be truly frustrating," she confirmed.

"You didn't have to agree so readily to my having shortcomings," he said wryly.

"I just want you to know that I don't look at you or the world through rose-colored glasses," she replied.

"That's good." Taking another step toward her, he reached out, took her hand and placed the necklace in it. "This is yours," he said, then reaching into his pocket, he pulled out a small jeweler's box. "And I'd like you to accept this, also."

Amanda laid the necklace and whistle on her dresser. With shaky hands, she took the box and opened it. Inside was a ring with a single yellow diamond.

"I can't promise you I'll ever be easy to live with," Hawk said gruffly. "But if you'll marry me, I *can* promise you I'll always be faithful and loyal, and I'll love you as strongly as any man has ever loved a woman."

Joy surged through her. "I've really never had a choice in this matter," she confessed with a crooked grin. "My instincts led me to you. And as hard as I've tried, I can't get you out of my heart. It's as if you're a part of me I needed to find and I don't feel whole unless I'm with you."

Looking like a man who has just been given his life back, Hawk scooped her up in his arms and kissed her with a passion that took her breath away.

Amanda awoke slowly. Drawing a deep, relaxing breath, she lay quietly. She felt content from the tips of her toes to the top of her head. She and Hawk had been married for a month today, and the bond she sensed with him grew stronger with each passing moment.

She smiled softly as she recalled his lovemaking of the night before. He'd proved to be not only an exciting lover but one who cared about her pleasure as much as his own. Who would have thought, she mused, that the tall, grim, intimidating stranger she'd met one night on the prairie would turn out to be the man for her. Needing to see him to reassure herself this wasn't all a dream, she turned to watch him sleep.

But Hawk was already awake, propped up on an elbow watching her. And the loving look in his eyes made her toes curl with delight.

"Good morning," she said softly, reaching out and stroking his jaw.

"Good morning," he replied, kissing her lightly as he combed a few wayward strands of hair from her face with his fingers.

His touch sent currents of ecstasy flowing through her. "It's a little frightening," she admitted, "how very much you mean to me."

He grinned with satisfaction, then said huskily, "That first night I found you out on the prairie, you scared the devil out of me. In the dark, you were more shadow than substance, yet I'd never felt such a strong attraction to a woman."

She frowned petulantly. "You were very good at hiding it. When Gloria offered me a job, I was sure you wanted to throw me off the ranch, instead."

"I did," he conceded. "I didn't feel safe with you around. Out on the prairie I'd tried telling myself my reaction was merely a trick of the moment. But all during that dinner, I was as aware of you as if you'd been sitting on my lap."

Amanda laughed. "Now that conjures up an interesting image."

He moved closer and ran his hand along her hip. "A very interesting image," he agreed.

His touch kindled the embers of desire. Lifting her head, Amanda kissed his shoulder. The warmth of his skin was intoxicating, and she smiled playfully as she lay back on her pillow. "We could try that the next time I need to lose weight. I'm sure you could keep my mind off Pauline's chocolate cake."

"I'd enjoy trying," he replied with a grin. Abruptly a shadow crossed his face and his expression became serious. "What frightens me is how close I came to losing you. I told myself that sending you away was the right thing to do. I wanted you to have the very best life possible. But after you left I'd wake up in a cold sweat from nightmares of you walking down the aisle with another man."

Reaching up, Amanda stroked his jaw again. "This is the very best life I could ever have," she assured him, adding honestly, "Before you came after me, I was beginning to worry that maybe I was doomed to spinsterhood. I don't think I could ever have married anyone but you."

An expression of pure pleasure spread over his face and he kissed her neck. "I should have known we were meant to be together, especially when Loco accepted you, allowing you to enter his corral to take care of his needs when I was sick. But I just told myself that he realized you were as stubborn and headstrong as he was and he respected you for that."

"Stubborn and headstrong?" she said with mock chagrin.

Mischief glistened in Hawk's eyes. "Just thought I should let you know I don't see you through rose-colored glasses, either."

Anxiety swept through Amanda. Was he feeling a twinge of regret at having married her? "And just how do you see me?" she asked.

"I see you as the perfect wife for me," he replied gruffly, his hand moving possessively along the curves of her body.

Relief spread through her. "I'm glad we both agree on that point."

Hawk looked hard into her face. "I will always be grateful to the fates that led you to me."

Amanda felt suddenly wrapped in a warmth so intense it could melt an iceberg. "My quest was amazingly successful," she conceded, trailing her hands over his chest as the fires of passion ignited within her. Drawing him down to her, she ran the tip of her tongue seductively along the taut cord of his neck. "Truly amazing," she murmured against his skin. Then all thought of conversation vanished as his mouth found hers and his touch became more intimate.

* * * * *

HE'S MORE THAN A MAN,
HE'S ONE OF OUR

CALEB'S SON
by Laurie Paige

Handsome widower Caleb Remmick had a business to run and a son to raise—alone. Finding help wasn't easy—especially when the only one offering was Eden Sommers. Years ago he'd asked for her hand, but Eden refused to live with his workaholic ways. Now his son, Josh, needed someone, and Eden was the only woman he'd ever trust—and the only woman he'd ever loved....

Look for *Caleb's Son* by Laurie Paige, available in March.

Fall in love with our **Fabulous Fathers!**

FF394

SPRING
Fancy
'94

They're sexy, single...
and about to get snagged!

Passion is in full bloom as love catches
the fancy of three brash bachelors. You won't
want to miss these stories by three of
Silhouette's hottest authors:

**CAIT LONDON
DIXIE BROWNING
PEPPER ADAMS**

Spring fever is in the air this March—
and there's no avoiding it!

Only from Silhouette®

where passion lives.

SF94

If you are looking for more titles by

ELIZABETH AUGUST

Don't miss this chance to order additional stories by
one of Silhouette's great authors:

Silhouette Romance™

#08809	A SMALL FAVOR	$2.50	☐
#08833	THE COWBOY AND THE CHAUFFEUR	$2.59	☐
#08857	LIKE FATHER, LIKE SON	$2.69	☐
#08881	THE WIFE HE WANTED	$2.69	☐
	The following titles are part of the Smytheshire, Massachusetts miniseries		
#08921	THE VIRGIN WIFE	$2.69	☐
#08922	HAUNTED HUSBAND	$2.69	☐
#08945	LUCKY PENNY	$2.75	☐
#08953	A WEDDING FOR EMILY	$2.75	☐

Men Made In America

#45158	AUTHOR'S CHOICE	$3.59	☐
	(limited quantities available on certain titles)		

TOTAL AMOUNT	$
POSTAGE & HANDLING	$
($1.00 for one book, 50¢ for each additional)	
APPLICABLE TAXES*	$_____
TOTAL PAYABLE	$_____
(check or money order—please do not send cash)	

To order, complete this form and send it, along with a check or money order
for the total above, payable to Silhouette Books, to: *In the U.S.*: 3010 Walden
Avenue, P.O. Box 9077, Buffalo, NY 14269-9077; *In Canada*: P.O. Box 636,
Fort Erie, Ontario, L2A 5X3.

Name: _____

Address: _____ City: _____

State/Prov.: _____ Zip/Postal Code: _____

*New York residents remit applicable sales taxes.
 Canadian residents remit applicable GST and provincial taxes.   EABACK2

Ⓥ *Silhouette* ®

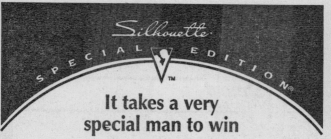

Silhouette SPECIAL EDITION

It takes a very special man to win

That SPECIAL *Woman!*

ONE LAST FLING!
Elizabeth August

Investigative reporter Max Laird never knew what hit him when he teamed up with Bernadette Dowd. After learning a shocking truth, Bernadette was determined to put some adventure and excitement in her life. Falling in love made them both realize what they had been missing...and that this wouldn't be just another fling for either of them!

Thrill to Bernadette's adventure in Elizabeth August's ONE LAST FLING!, available in March.

She's friend, wife, mother—she's you! And beside each Special Woman stands a wonderfully *special* man. It's a celebration of our heroines—and the men who become part of their lives.

Don't miss **THAT SPECIAL WOMAN!** each month— from some of your special authors! Only from Silhouette Special Edition!

Relive the romance...
Harlequin and Silhouette
are proud to present

A program of collections of three complete novels by the most requested authors with the most requested themes. Be sure to look for one volume each month with three complete novels by top name authors.

In January: **WESTERN LOVING**   Susan Fox
                                     JoAnn Ross
                                     Barbara Kaye

Loving a cowboy is easy—taming him isn't!

In February: **LOVER, COME BACK!**   Diana Palmer
                                         Lisa Jackson
                                         Patricia Gardner Evans

It was over so long ago—yet now they're calling, "Lover, Come Back!"

In March: **TEMPERATURE RISING**   JoAnn Ross
                                       Tess Gerritsen
                                       Jacqueline Diamond

Falling in love—just what the doctor ordered!

Available at your favorite retail outlet.

REQ-G3

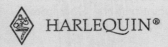

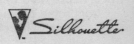